Consequences of the Battle
at Sandy Creek

by

Neil Thomas

ISBN 978-0-9865914-1-9

Acknowledgment

This book wouldn't have been written without having read first Doug McCalla's excellent textbook Planting the Province: The Economic History of Upper Canada 1784-1870 (University of Toronto Press). An early version of this manuscript served as input to the Summer's Writing School at Humber College in 1998; thank you to Timothy Findley, Bill Whitehead and others who commented on the draft. There was (as far as I know) no body such as the King's Border Scouts nor the Sacket Rangers. Cartwright, Macdonell, Chauncey, Armstrong and Yeo, and the latters' underlings, were real historical characters, and conducted most of the war as described, though fiction has demanded that I make certain events different from how they would have seen them. The Battle of Sandy Creek did occur; other names, including some places, have been changed. There was one person largely responsible for funding the ironworks mentioned here, including the production of cannonball.

The Golden Sword (*Espada Dorada*) is my substitute nom-de-guerre for a movement (Shining Path – Sendero Luminoso) that I believe was culpable in my friend Barbara d'Achille's death in Peru in the 1980s..

The use of real names, other than those identified, is entirely coincidental. Thanks to St Lawrence Cruise Lines for the use of their map in deriving mine, and Meghan Thomas for her help.

For my wife, Ana.

Table of Contents

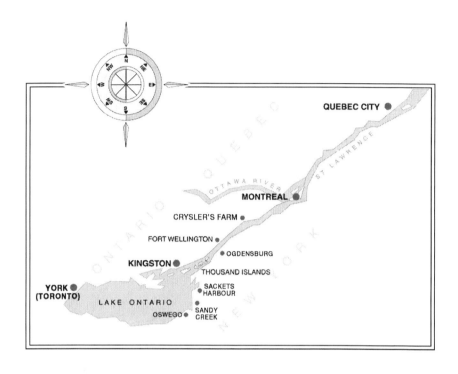

Map of where it all happened.

Prologue

They made it a ceremonial departure from Sackets Harbor, the oars of the gunboat sweeping in time to the beat of a drum. He had not intended to look at anyone standing on land, but the vessel swung with the touch of the onshore breeze against the bow, and his sight, in his effort to avoid looking the coxswain directly in the face, was directed over the coxswain's shoulder. Chauncey himself stood there on the shore, with a Captain of Dragoons beside him.

He recognized the Captain, of course. He wondered what the Captain's role had been. The gloating on the Captain's face caused the bottom suddenly to fall out of his stomach.

Once clear of the harbour, the commanding lieutenant gave the bosun the course and ordered the sails run up. The gunboat lurched forward as the crew shipped their oars. They settled into a rhythm of rising and falling as the swells ran under them, the breeze strong enough to lay the gunboat a little on her side. The crew, talking amongst themselves, seemed to be taking care not to include him in their comments, nor, in the case of the coxswain, who was the only crew member aft of him, to look at him.

He knew not, clearly, what was about to happen. He had languished in their gaol for two days, fed on little but the taunts of his gaoler, and then, at daybreak, had been marched to the water's edge. The gunboat had been waiting, oars out, and barely had the lieutenant acknowledged receipt of him as his prisoner than he had ordered the vessel to cast off.

At one point he'd made the motion of turning to look forward, but the lieutenant called ` Prisoner, eyes astern!'. Turning back, he met the coxswain's eyes briefly, but they were as empty as the horizon. One of the crew laughed; the bosun chastised him.

As the gunboat raced on, his thoughts slipped back into the turmoil of the previous days. There had been death in volumes far greater than he'd ever seen before. In relative terms, that of his few friends paled in comparison to the slaughter at Sandy Creek, but the latter had been people he hadn't known so his real pain lay with his friends. By their deaths he had stepped off the edge of the earth, into an abyss of horror. By itself it was so terrible that he had not initially made any reading of it, suffering just the fact. But as the first night passed and daylight brought a hardening to the edges of all the images awash in his mind, he began to see evil. Evil that seemed to go beyond the simple necessity of causing death. All his friends must have died in great pain. That, more than anything, was what he was unable to understand. *Why?* His stomach said that the Captain had something to do with it.

The lieutenant's call: `Run up the white flag,' brought him out of his reverie. Even though he'd been wrapped in terrible thoughts he had noted the course, and had been watching the land passing, and knew that they were heading for the head of the river; this made it almost certain that they would shortly be in British waters, perhaps were so already. Perhaps even when he saw that he was to be ferried away he'd understood that this was to be a delivery, though the thought had not formed itself clearly. But his ensuing ostracism enforced the idea - he was already apart from them. A white flag was a flag of truce; but he, as prisoner, was to be no part of any formal discourse.

They passed a few small vessels, whose crews looked at their passage with curiosity. Over the stern he saw the occasional arm point towards them. News was no slouch in its travel, but he had no idea whether the catastrophe at Sandy Creek was yet common knowledge. If it were, perhaps, on top of the news of two weeks before at Oswego, people were beginning to think that they could not win a battle, that the war was going to wear them away little by little. It would be no good news for Sir James, that Popham had lost him perhaps a third of the men fresh from Britain. A third of *those* were perhaps already beneath unfamiliar soil.

`Ready, now!' called the bosun. The coxswain's eyes scanned the waters ahead, watching he knew not what, and he sensed the crew become more alert. Wolfe island was to starboard, smoke from someone's fire drifting above the trees and then swept east on the wind. `Keep her to windward,' the lieutenant called, and the gunboat passed an armed schooner at anchor in the roads above Kingston. `Good-day to you, sir,' the lieutenant shouted, and he saw the head of an officer on the vessel's poop. Even though he must have seen the flag, he'd heard the clacking of opening gunports, evidence that gunboats were to be respected, as was surprise.

The Kingston shore turned up into the mouth of the Cataraqui, but they held their course towards Navy Island. Behind him, he heard shouts on land, though he doubted that they'd just been seen - the semaphores would have been indicating for more than half an hour now, passing the news as *they* passed. The schooner had already run up some signal flags.

`Drop sails.....oars out.' The crew had been ready, and there was the rattle of the falling mainsail, which was quickly gathered and tied. The oars went out, the bosun muttering `let's do this well, boys, show them whose navy *this* is....' though the lieutenant kept quiet and they drifted slowly on the water.

A few moments later he called `American gunboat *Desperance,* under flag of truce, Lieutenant Colway commanding, requests permission to approach mooring.'

But there was already the sound of oars pulling hard through the water and his request was very quickly denied. `Gunboat *Desperance*, you will hold your position. Do not approach point.'

`Someone doesn't want us to see what's round there on the slips,' laughed one of the crew behind him. `As if we didn't already know.'

`Quiet, Layton,' ordered the bosun, and there was the sound of someone sucking his teeth in disgust.

A different gunboat appeared in the corner of his vision, circling them. `Gunboat *Desperance*, would you state your purpose in entering British waters?'

`I am commanded by Commodore Isaac Chauncey, Commander of the United States Navy at Sackets Harbor, to deliver unto Sir James Yeo, Commander of the British Fleet at Kingston, one prisoner.'

`A prisoner?'

The lieutenant must have gestured, for he felt most of the eyes in the British gunboat focus on him. `We have arrested him as a spy. The details of his arrest, and the damage he has caused the British Fleet, you will find in this despatch. Please be so good as to deliver it to your Commodore.'

He heard someone say `bastard!' `Quiet in the boat!' roared the British Officer, who was standing in the bow beside the gun. The gunboat had slowly moved to face them bow on, even though they were under a flag of truce, and the muzzle of her cannon was no more than twenty-five yards away beyond their stern. It was a cautious move, leaving the American gunboat's cannon pointed out over open water. `Ship your starboard oars,' the British Officer called.

`Do as he says, boys,' said the bosun. `He's coming alongside.' Then, `on your feet, prisoner.'

The muzzle of the gun came ever closer until the bow actually scraped the American gunwhale. 'Hold her there, bosun,' called the British Officer to his own boat captain. 'Let's be having him, then.'

He was shoved hard by someone who'd also stood behind him. The lieutenant had come aft and was passing a packet with a large wax seal across to his British counterpart. He opened a small travelling case. 'Kindly sign this receipt.' An arm reached up and pulled him across onto the British vessel. He was made to stand beside the officer, who looked at him carefully.

'Proof you didn't drop him overboard, eh?'

The American lieutenant was solemn. 'Oh, we thought an American drowning was too good for him. Better a British rope.' He took back his receipt, and stowed it in the case beside the quill and inkpot. 'Permission to depart?'

The British officer nodded. 'Good day to you, sir. A good voyage home.' Then, to his own bosun: 'Put him somewhere where he won't fall overboard before we get him on dry land.' And, 'I wonder who he is?'

Sir James had had no reason to set eyes on him before, so the prisoner looked for the first time into that cautious mind. Rather, he sensed its presence, for the prisoner's eyes were on the King, hanging in portraiture on the wall behind. Yeo was reading the despatch, and making frequent sounds of dismay. 'Popham is at least alive, then,' he commented to an naval officer standing by his side. 'Here's his letter.' He waved it, then settled down to read it. 'Ah, Spilsbury too. Good.'

After a while he put the papers on his desk and he felt his gaze upon him. 'Lieutenant!'

'Sir.'

'I do not like what I have read.'

'No, sir.'

'What have you to say?'

'I have not seen the despatches, sir. I cannot respond to their contents.'

It made Yeo angry. 'I should not think it necessary for you to read them. It's what you've done that I'm talking about. Popham's loss.'

8

The idea was dawning on him that he had been cast into serious trouble. 'I had nothing to do with it, sir.' The Captain of Dragoons was not to be drawn into it, yet.

'You were there.'

'I was taken to watch, sir.'

Yeo picked up the despatch. 'Commodore Chauncey states that you were apprehended in flight.'

'No, sir. I was apprehended on the Superior as I boarded her.'

'You boarded the Superior?' He was unable to hide his surprise.

'To count her guns, sir.'

'Lieutenant. I cannot believe that Commodore Chauncey would lie. He says nothing about your boarding.'

'Then he has not lied, sir.'

His voice was cutting. 'Do not play games with me, Lieutenant! Rather too many men have died for that.'

'I am unable to offer any defence if I do not know what I am accused of, sir.'

'What were you doing over there?'

'Collecting intelligence, sir.'

'For whom?'

'Colonel Cartwright, sir.'

'Cartwright? The merchant?' It came out with a touch of disdain. To a professional officer, Mr Richard's military appointment appeared not to compete with his trade.

'Yes, sir.'

'Why would he want to know how many guns were on the Superior?'

'That was not my main task, sir.'

'No? Well, whatever it was, Lieutenant, the Americans think you will want to answer to a charge of treason. What say you to that?'

'I can say nothing, sir.' He thought that once Yeo had talked with Mr Richard, perhaps the whole matter could be clarified.

'I'd better talk to Cartwright, I suppose. But,' he picked up the despatch and waved it, 'this is a case strongly made. I don't doubt you *will* be court-martialled.'

In his cell, when he could put aside the images of his friends, his thoughts continually went back to Popham and his men, night after night. Perhaps the *keplunk-keplunk* of a bittern undisturbed in the rushes to starboard suggested that the shores of the creek were as quiet as fleeing small craft would have left them. There was no doubt that the pursuers were emboldened by visions of glory in an American May morning, though it was glory that would detract from American interests, and might, were the result as originally hoped, have affected the outcome of the whole war differently.

But glory can be akin to foolhardiness, leading men to take risk in situations where caution might have been a better bet. And if command itself has no clear vision of how to build victory, but ebbs and flows with the wind and water which it believes are its only tools, risk takes on a different form. And on that May morning, the risk had been considerable.

Whether a bittern made that enticing sound, or even an Indian of the defending force, was a possibility never considered in the ensuing enquiry.

Joinery

In an extraordinary act of rural violence three people died that day. Extraordinary, because no death is like another; extraordinary, because it was my fault.

I remember Carlos' admonishment, that I was mad. He'd said so every time I saw him, but he'd said it with the feeling of friendship and genuine worry. But I got as far as I did because of his help, his sharing the resources of his network of rural wool-buyers to find the sort of community I wanted. And it had been his cable that had said he'd finally done it, but that if I failed to show up he couldn't promise the same in the future.

I know very little about wool. Through Carlos I understood that not only does it come from sheep but also from the more exotic alpaca, an animal which looks like a sheep that has undergone severe neck and leg traction. A small camel, said Carlos, each worth a small fortune. So wool was only on the fringes of my mind. Though, because of Carlos, it was key to what I did and how I did it.

Carlos is a proud man, descendant of a line of wool merchants. In his physiognomy are the marks of the aristocracy of both the English Midlands and the Spanish Extremadura, blue eyes over a hawk's nose. His family is one of the leaders of the Peruvian alpaca industry, so he knows the altiplano like the back of his hand and also the animals that graze it.

But now he stays as close to home as possible. ` *Peligrosísimo*, Alastair, extremely dangerous. I would be a prime mark for these people you seek, so I am afraid that most of my buying is now done here. But my men still travel between the communities. I will tell them what you want, and they will let me know.' Here, was the *hacienda*, the remains of the family property that had escaped the land reforms of past decades, and in whose warehouses was the intake of rolls of alpaca fleece, the grading and sorting rooms, and the baling of the sorted wool. The locks on the doors behind which was stored the baby alpaca, the prime fleece, were far smaller though much more modern than those where the remaining wool was kept. Those looked as though they had come across the Atlantic with Pizarro, almost five hundred years ago.

So my companion had been Carlos' man, one of his wool scouts who took price news out and supply news back, and who then arranged the contracts. He had been worried on two accounts. Firstly, that my presence might sour future relations with this village, which was one of his sources. Secondly, that the news might reach those ultimate ears that he had been the intermediary, with who-knew-what consequences. I felt sorry for him, but for the moment I needed him. For it would be on the strength of the respect they held for him that the villagers would take me on the next step.

'*No se preocupe*, Pedro, don't worry so much. Once they agree to take me, your job is finished. You can tell Señor Estrada that you accomplished your part in this.' Carlos was Señor Estrada, and he would be very keen to know exactly what happened. Which was why I knew what Pedro was going to say.

'Señor Estrada, *señor*, will want me to stay with you. He will not forgive me if I don't accompany you on the rest of your mission.'

But the battle was clear on his face, so I tore a sheet of paper from my notebook and scribbled a note on it. 'Give this to Señor Estrada. It says the village refused to take you.'

So when the decision was finally made, and I set off with a new guide, Pedro did not accompany us. But I hadn't told a lie. They had refused to take him. Though the reason was clear: as their conduit to cash income from wool, Pedro was a thousand times more valuable to them than was I. He, they wanted to keep alive.

There had been no doubt that the man just a step away was a killer. It started with the pig eyes in a nearly bloated face, made slightly crimson by the tight collar. But it had nothing to do with an unreliable stereotype, rather that his uniform stated the fact, and the knowledge that his men had just summarily executed eleven villagers for only suspicion of something that was illegal. This wasn't the official story, of course, but general knowledge in the town said that there had been no attempt to prove any allegation, and the raiding troop had just become fed up with lying confessions induced under torture so had shot them all. It had happened before and would happen again.

'*No, señor. No hay ningún problema de seguridad en la zona.*' No, there's no security problem in this region.

I'd had to see him before Carlos would let me go. '*Sí*, I will help you, Alastair, you know that. But I have to observe propriety, and propriety here says that you must pay respect, even if you have none.'

As a foreign journalist I'd had to learn the official story, blatantly untrue. Especially when ordinary peasants went in fear of their lives from their own protectors. But the military in Latin America tends to be the last bastion of the Inquisition, even if it lacks the divine right the church assumed centuries before. So in this case the Peruvian military, under *General* Pablo López Martín, of the Second Cavalry, *Brigada Andina*, used terminal force to protect his Government's reputation in dealing with terrorism. Even though, in this case, the dead had probably had no links with the terrorists. The equanimity in his voice was a betrayal of basic human rights.

Most peasants have nothing to do with the terrorists if they have any choice in the matter. To be visited by the *Espada Dorada,* the Golden Sword, is a death wish, and all peasants fervently wish to live, even in the close-to-abject poverty ensured by the High Andes. But the *Espada* is continually on the move, especially at night, and it was inevitable that most isolated communities would at one time or another be blighted. The effects of that blight had resulted in mass migration into larger communities, adding further to the effects of poverty. As far as the military was concerned it was a matter of reputation, a demonstration of a lack of weakness, to scorch the earth as viciously as the *Espada*. To fight fear with fear. Only the greater fear could win.

`But, *General*, have you taken any *Espada* encampments in the last year? Have you managed to seize any arms?'

`We have been gloriously successful, *señor*. We have rid the *puna* of this vermin. They are afraid to meet my gallant cavalry, and so disappear into the *selva* far below.'

The truth was two hundred peasants dead, none proven to be *Espadinos*, and about forty troops with their throats slit at night, in the last year alone. But soldiers were as expendable as peasants, so success wasn't measured in terms of achievements without death, but rather by disparity in numbers. Heaven help the local population if the number of deceased troopers were to approach civilian casualties.

At no time during the interview did *Generalísimo* Pablo, as Carlos called him, directly answer any of my questions. I hadn't really expected him to, but he'd known I was coming, had known that I had to see him so that he could give official blessing to my presence in his military region. So I gave him his opportunity to wash his hands of me.

`I would like to visit some of the rural communities where the *Espada* has been.'

`*Usted sabe, señor*, you know that I cannot give you any protection if you insist on travelling outside the city. You may be at great risk. The Andes are not kind to foreigners - many meet with accidents every year. The *puna* is a hard place.'

I thought it curious, if all the *Espadinos* had hared off to the lowland jungle, the *selva* he had mentioned, that he thought I should still need protection on the outskirts of town.' Then, *General*, I will assume the responsibility for my own risks. Thank you for warning me of the dangers.'

The pig eyes didn't blink, but the oil in the voice turned rancid. ' *Señor* MacNeil. Do not be a foolish man. They have killed others such as you. Foreign journalists are not welcomed by these people. You are seen to be part of the Establishment they fight against, and the lead of their bullet will be as bitter to you as it is to any of my soldiers. Why should they spare you?'

It was as close to an admission of his failure as I was likely to get, though I was not going to point this out. ' *General*, I value your advice and thank you for it. I will take as few risks as possible.' Certainly fewer, I thought, than the peasants in those communities where his men posed as locals, waiting to sound the alarm. The *Espadinos* took them out first, ensuring official retribution for the hapless citizenry left behind. No, I certainly didn't want his protection, even knowing that there were many *Espadinos* much closer than the *selva* he suggested was their present home.

He shrugged, and then dismissed me with a slight movement of his right hand in the direction of the exit. Even though he picked up a paper off his desk with a show of intending to read it, the pig eyes were in the centre of my back for every step I took to, and past, the dark hardwood door that protected his sanctuary. For a moment I felt that, beyond it, I was as much in danger from him as I was from his political foe.

Signals are bitter things, if you miss them. And *Generalísimo* Pablo gave me a clear one. But I chose to ignore it, and went about my business like the fool Carlos always thought I was. Later, I wondered about the Andean telegraph, how the word had moved so fast, but in reality I'd taken my time getting there, so they could have waved flags in the dark and still the message would have arrived sooner than I did.

I thought it was the full moon, a massive disc of light in my eyes, and wanted to turn over in the warmth of my high-altitude sleeping bag and fall back into a still-oxygen-starved sleep, which was full of images, in the main blood-red. The boot in the ribs shattered that, and something very cold and hard pressed deep into my ear brought a sense of being utterly alone and imminently on the road to eternity.

At first there were no words spoken, just the continuous pressure of the gun barrel and a hand that felt its way over the whole surface of the sleeping bag, searching. Then another hard kick, and, ' *Levantate.*' Get up.

The gun barrel didn't move, but the body stepped back and the movements of the flashlight brought two other shadows into the night, equally armed. I have never moved so slowly and carefully, and I edged my way out of the sleeping bag. Then I stood up.

`Que es eso? What is this? Why do we have a foreigner here in this territory? Who is he? Contesta!' The command brought a blow to my guide's stomach from a gunstock, and he doubled over in pain.

`A visitor, capitán.'

`Fool! I can see he's a visitor. His skin is not the same colour as yours, is it? He looks like an americano. What's he doing here?' The blow was repeated.

`He asked that I bring him, capitán. He wanted to see some communities, talk to some people.'

`What did he want to talk about? Who is he? Who sent him?'

`I cannot tell you much more, capitán. I only brought him here today.'

`Then we shall have to ask him, shan't we?'

The light hadn't moved from my face, so I couldn't see any detail of the men standing in the dark. But their Spanish was different from the gentle song-like tones of the Qechua peasants - a harder, more precise lowland diction. I thought the capitán from my guide was just a mark of respect for someone who held all the cards, and not an acknowledgement of prior familiarity and superior status.

As the gunbarrel was closer, that was what hit me in the stomach, a sharp blow just under the sternum. `So. Who are you?"

`Just a visitor.'

`What are you doing here?' Even harder this time, taking the edge off my breathing, leaving me gasping.

`Seeing how people cope with thugs like you.'

I don't know why I said it. A loss of control in a moment of pain, perhaps. There was only one outcome, the gunstock swinging around in the dark to take me across the side of the head. When I was on the ground, the boot came back in.

`Well, you can learn at first hand. When they are insolent, we treat them like this.'

It lasted about thirty seconds. Thirty seconds that became infinite intervals of time between blows. Nothing more to the head, but to the ribs and back, ever more exposed as the body sought foetal refuge.

`Stand him up. Against that wall, there. Our visitor will have the pleasure of seeing it coming. A gift from the *Espada Dorada*. *Viva la revolución*!'

I could see the knees of my hosts as they dragged me up against the wall. The woman's were shaking, and the husband's sagging in despair. The guide stood stoically, head erect, staring into the void of incomprehensible violence. The light slipped a little and I saw into the faces of my captors, but they were masked, no features visible beyond the eyes.

`*Lo siento mucho, señora*.' But she was beyond hearing, seeing into her own future as she had done that afternoon, and no words of any apology of mine were going to change anything. Her husband's eyes were filled with tears.

And after they did what they did, they beat me senseless. A clear signal - one, when I came around, which I understood fully.

I don't know who found me. Carlos said later that they brought me down to the hacienda on a litter slung between two llamas. They'd thought I was dead at first, because the other bodies had been piled on top of me, and their blood had drenched my clothing. It had formed a six hour crust before they pulled us apart. I was glad that I had not wakened to the embrace and gaze of my dead hosts.

Under the care of Graciela, Carlos' wife, I was cleaned up and put to bed in one of the downstairs rooms immediately adjacent to Carlos' study. Apparently, I remained unconscious for twelve hours, and barely exhibited sentience for the following twenty-four. Then the pain started to creep in and the body began to complain. At some point I was given a draught which knocked me out for another day. Then officialdom wanted its due. `*Ahora tienes que despertarte*, Alastair'. Now you must wake up. `The police wish to talk to you.' A maid helped me to sip a hot *mate de coca*.

I thought it a room that had probably seen many generations of Estradas, perhaps in conditions not much different from mine. Large, with enormous black beams spanning the width of the ceiling, it had the look of a place where the current patriarch of the family would be brought in his final hours to be helped across into a beneficent Catholic afterlife, surrounded by all who wished to witness the event. A large crucifix hung over the head of the bed, and a very old painting of the Virgin Mary blessed the wall beyond my feet. The windows were heavily curtained, but even though the floor was a dark stone, it glowed from its patina of wax.

The *mate* insinuated itself through some of the gaps of memory, and sealed them sufficiently for me to understand *why* the police wished to talk to me. I found myself awake, with the first full understanding of where I was since I recalled walking with a guide across the *puna*.

'*Señor* MacNeil.' There were three of them, a senior officer and two adjutants. The officer looked as if he'd just come from the hippodrome, and his helpers were no less groomed. 'I am sorry to hear what happened. You are fortunate to be alive.'

He was too courteous. I didn't understand it at first, but then I saw that this man was from Lima, no local police flunky. I looked across at Carlos, who was standing in the shadows of the curtained window. He perhaps saw my puzzlement. '*Coronel* Patricio Suarez is an old friend of mine, Alastair. The local police commandant was kind enough to allow him to be the first to talk to you.' He gestured, and then I saw a fourth man, similarly uniformed though quite differently dressed, and whose face spoke more to local bloodlines. He kept his distance from the *Limeños*.

It took me a long time to tell my story through still swollen lips. Initial disjointed thoughts coalesced slowly into the picture of what had happened, completed by Carlos' description of the bloodbath. There were moments in which I was unable to say what I remembered, the events coming back into my mind with such force that I despaired of finding the ability, let alone the words, to describe what I'd done.

Coronel Suarez asked no more than a couple of questions. I wondered if Carlos had brought him in to distance both him and me from the local authorities, though once Suarez seemed to have finished he turned to the local commandant. '*Algo más, Mayor?*' Anything more, Major?

'*Un nombre, señor?*' A name? 'Did you hear anything said which might have been significant?'

'I'm afraid there is much I still do not remember. Perhaps some will come back with time.'

'Of course, *señor*. We can talk again once you are better. But please remember that the sooner we look for these people, the sooner we may catch them.'

But the hours before darkness had been beaten into me were still hazy, and I could remember little of any of the conversation. Though I knew that it was no conversation ever to want to remember beyond any purpose of justice. At the moment, it was no more than threads, isolated phrases. 'Capitán.'

'*Si, señor?*' One of the adjutants came quickly to attention.

'No, no. I meant 'capitán', a name. The guide called the leader by that term. I thought it was just a mark of respect.' Respect driven by fear was how I'd read it.

Suarez looked at the commandant. 'Capitán? Does it signify anything?'

The commandant moved not a muscle, gazing through me as if thinking deeply, then turned to Suarez. 'I believe not, *Coronel.*' But he said no more.

Suarez looked at him briefly, then shrugged. 'Very well. *Señor* MacNeil, I think you will be staying where you are for a few days. If I can, I shall visit you once again before you depart, though we may better be able to arrange that meeting when you pass through Lima.' I am a busy man, he meant, and only attend to foolish foreigners out of friendship for others.

'Thank you, *Coronel.*'

'*Sí, Patricio. Gracias.*' Carlos came out of his shadow, taking Suarez' hand, and shaking it as the group left the room.

The commandant followed a little behind, turning to me before passing through the doorway. 'Perhaps you will also visit me, *señor*, so that we may think a little, together?'

I thought his mind as knifelike as Suarez' was languid. 'Of course, *Mayor*. I will contact you through Carlos.'

He nodded without speaking, and left.

Carlos came back after a further ten minutes or so, enough for me to have slipped back into a doze. I came back to consciousness to find him standing over the bed.

'Did you really hear that word spoken?'

'You think I dreamt it somewhere during the last couple of days?'

'No, Alastair. I think probably not. I am concerned for its ramifications.'

I was as well aware of them as he. 'I felt a fool saying it.'

'You may not be a fool to think it, Alastair, but you would be a fool to say it aloud again anywhere around here.'

I lay in that bed for a further two days. Looking back, there was nothing in me to encourage any sort of movement towards mental or physical recovery. I lay there in anguish, a continual burning despair at myself for what I had brought to pass, and hate at the forces of death which I had harnessed. In the end Carlos forced me out of the bed, saying he required my presence with his family at dinner - purple, yellow and black face or no. I'd given no thought to how I looked, so I was surprised to hear the description. He nodded. 'It'll clear up twice as fast if you get up and move about. And the rest of you will probably require the same thing.' He pointed at my knees, which still ached from the beating.

But he was cognizant enough of my shame to let me do it in my own time.

' I am a decent man and do not wish any of these thugs well. Hear me, *señor,* I said *any.*'

I'd limped into Tarrasco's office, Carlos having advised him that I was able to walk. ' Tell him to bring his memories,' the commandant had said to Carlos. Carlos recounted it to me. ' Remember what we said, Alastair.'

Mayor Felipe Tarrasco fitted his office better than he fitted the uniform his coastal peers had worn that first visit. The office was like a carpenter's bench, worn and stained. Looking at it as I sat down I suddenly had the feeling that from it came works of art. I see good police work as no different from joinery, but it takes a master to cut the dovetails to fit. So if there were any clues lying there in my mind, or in that slaughterhouse of a hut, the right mind would be able to place them in the whole. I think I saw it in his eyes, obsidian of an ancient race, that afternoon when he'd shrugged off any reaction the *Limeños* might have had to his reading of that single word. *This is my field, not theirs, no matter what the Coronel may owe your friend.*

So I suddenly knew that we would not be dealing with anything as simple as a statement. In that office I was to be held against the light, grain checked for swirl, before he decided how best to use me in the cabinet he was making of this case. He'd want more than just a leg; he'd want a finished piece, French polished.

' Let me make it quite clear, *señor* MacNeil. I am dealing with evil here, and your story is one of several in which equally filthy deeds were done. The other day I heard you tell a story; today I wish you to retell that story, but you will take your time, and you will tell me everything. This is not a threat; it is the request of one decent man to another.'

So we went through it all, even what I had talked about with the peasants, and who had been in attendance. It had been my local guide who had called the man ' *capitán*', and while I weighed Carlos' words carefully, there was in Tarrasco something that gave me the confidence to say what I thought.

He looked into and through me as he had done during the first visit. ' That is precisely why you and I are in this office alone, *señor* MacNeil. Now describe him to me.'

19

So, unlike before, I brought the man to life in my mind, and described every detail of him I could remember. Surprisingly, the mask he had been wearing became irrelevant, even slipped, as I dragged out things I hadn't even known I'd seen. He ceased to exist as just a physical object - rather, he became movement, and in movement is being.

Nodding, Tarrasco sat back in his chair and examined his ceiling. `Perhaps the secret in description is to be not of our people.' Then, apparently also approving of what he saw above him, his eyes came back to mine. `I will ask a very great favour of you, *señor*. I wish to catch this man and his comrades. Will you help me?'

The knowledge of what he asked became a blanket of ice wrapping my whole body. But there was also a great sense of futility. `What good will it do to catch them. Will justice be done?'

`And if I guarantee justice, *señor*? If I promise that at least the crime you witnessed will be paid for, and in full?'

`In full?' The qualifier had been important, because it added a dimension I needed him to understand.

`If *you* will help me, yes.'

But, though dead of heart for what I had brought to three people, and angrier still at the greater crime, I found I could not give my consent even if some sense of honour demanded it. Tarrasco's suggestion made me afraid for my life.

He sat immobile in his chair as I left.

Carlos told me, subsequently, that, since our acquaintance, it was the first sensible thing I'd done.

Toronto's office towers crowded the sky, clouds reflected in window glass doing nothing to soften hard, unfeeling edges. I looked out of one of those windows, feeling hemmed in, wishing I could see far to the south. The voice came from a man seated at his desk.

`You will have to get over it, Alastair. I think the guilt will be with you a long time, but don't you think many more will go the same way before it is all over?'

It was no comfort that Jack posed it as a question. I felt like ice, no feeling at all, except this overwhelming bitterness at myself and at what I'd done. Now that the event was broadly known, others were saying the same as Jack, though some others had said very much unkinder things which were much closer to my own thoughts. If Carlos had understood my mental devastation, he had been more concerned that I recover physically first. They had left me very close to death, but to my mind not quite close enough. I looked down to the street far below, waiting for vertigo to take me into free fall. But nothing happened.

'For the moment I *cannot* write about this.'

'Why?' Jack was unforgiving, as a newspaper editor has to be.

'Because I can only see it. I can't *feel* it.' But I didn't want to. I thought that if ever I was able to feel again, those feelings *would* kill me. There seemed to be nothing else ever to consider, to have feelings about.

'Then take some time off. Your last piece will come out in four weeks. I'll leave you another month to write the follow-up. Remember, *this* was what you were heading for, whether you knew it or not, and you owe us this story. I won't hold what we have in hand or we'll lose the momentum of it all. You've *got* to write it, Alastair. It *has* to be told.'

I could see his logic, and it meant money, after all. He sold his paper on the basis of quality journalism, and we'd worked a long time to build this story, to make the contacts, and build the expectation in the readership of firsthand knowledge, directly from where it was happening. That's what I'd wanted to deliver, why I'd done what I'd done. Now I didn't know how to handle it. Suddenly, I was a small boy lost. Suddenly, I needed to talk to Grandmother.

'Go and do something else for a couple of weeks, Alastair. Get some fresh air, a change of scenery. Kingston, perhaps.' He knew I had no relations to stay with, apart from Grandmother, so didn't make the mistake of saying anything trite. He'd known me long enough to know in the past that he'd find me in Kingston if he needed to talk to me. He was as considerate as he was tough. 'Or go out west, or something.'

His phone rang and he turned to pick it up. The conversation was over anyway, so I walked towards the door, not listening to his end of the current dialogue.

'Alastair. *Alastair!*'

As I'd stopped listening, I'd missed his first call.

'What?'

'Oh Jesus Christ...' he showed a sudden devastation. 'I...'

'Come on, Jack. I was just off out west, or somewhere.'

His head dropped. 'This is terrible.'

21

`Something happened?'

`Yes, it has.'

`Peru?'

`No. Kingston.'

`Kingston?'

`Your grandmother. I'm afraid she just died.'

Of course, I didn't believe him immediately. Had it been true, I thought, I would have had an instant upwelling of grief - might even have known, before he'd said it, that she was already gone. But nothing came, and I started to tell Jack that I thought it was a joke in very bad taste. I didn't complete the criticism, though, for my knees gave way and I was suddenly and violently sick.

'Good,' said Jack, once I'd made a complete mess of his carpet, 'now you know that you can feel something, even,' and he showed a touch of the cynical perspicacity he was known for, 'if you thought everything was completely frozen.' He smiled sadly. 'I'm sorry it has taken this to do it.'

I hobbled to one of his chairs as he said it, and sat doubled over, hands clasped across the massive cramp in my stomach. If Grandmother truly were dead then I really was lost, because in her I had hoped to find some peace, her wisdom that much older than mine.

Grandmother

I took the train to Kingston - the Montrealer. Like most Canadian trains, this one still spoke of a past age of railway, a sombre uniform on its conductor, and more staff and less speed than I thought modern business practice would find profitable. It brought the image of the Cuzco-to-Puno train to mind, a journey which takes you out of a city at once both Incan and post-colonial Peruvian, and into one lying on the shores of a lake so large that ancient and rusted steamers (brought up in pieces, also by railway) still try and cross it daily to Bolivia. The Montrealer wended its way along the shores of Lake Ontario until it reached Trenton, but I could as easily have been crossing the fringes of Lake Titicaca on the last leg into Puno.

The motion rocked me into a time of all times, thinking about Grandmother and the last ten years, thinking about what she had given me, and why we had liked each other. During the time we had shared, I had travelled for her, become her suitcase. From me she unpacked and filled a life left vacant by uncaring children, still extant somewhere else in the world but never willing to spend the money on an airfare or two in any of the last three decades. I was their offspring, of course, but a chance decision to take a postgraduate course at Queen's, a place hated by parents who had grown up in its shadow, had brought me into touch with the old woman just as my grandfather created a larger void in her life by his own dying.

I'd not known my grandfather beyond a toddler's memories of a smoky old man, pipesmoke, wreaths of it. Until I met my grandmother again I thought he had been a pipefitter, no pun intended, just an inaccurate description of his craft by his disinterested daughter. She had the knack of putting him down as far as she could, elevating herself in the process, not caring that he'd been an independent inventor, brilliant at taking anything out of three-dimensional space and making it work in somebody's industrial process. He liked his work-clothes, had his best ideas in them, so was not a snobbish daughter's idea of a perfect father, hands also generally not spotless, and so she had refused to go to Queen's because of it. Working class, she thought they'd think her, in what she saw as those still fusty halls.

But I'd had the curiosity of one long from shores that rang in memory as home, so had left my parents to an increasingly alcoholic itinerance, and had come to meet my grandmother.

Then the lake came and went as we rounded the Bay of Quinte, and I saw little more of it on the rest of the journey. I dozed a little during the last half hour, and only came awake with the conductor's call as the train slowed past Collins Bay.

I walked into town from the station, a long walk which a taxi would have cut to ten minutes. But I was still in the past, and something in me wanted to finish that process of cataloguing and wrapping memories before I reached my destination. A taxi would have brought indecent haste. So I went on remembering, not really thinking about or seeing anything around me, but I had not touched on even a fraction of what she had been to me before I found myself on more familiar ground. I turned the corner into her street, what had been her street, and somehow I thought that perhaps the house wouldn't be there, that she'd have taken it with her. But of course she hadn't, and the sight of the mellow gray limestone surrounding those multiple-paned windows brought a searing catch at the back of the throat. Then I knew I would never see her face at them again, and I cried.

The elderly figure who opened the door to me looked at me briefly, past the tears, and when he was sure it was me, turned back into the house leaving me to close the door behind us. ` I am sorry for your grief, Mr MacNeil. She was a fine woman to you just as you were such a grandson to her. You will miss her.'

He was dry, slightly pedantic, but I knew that even Lacroix would be feeling something. He'd been her solicitor for more than fifty years, and her passing would be a milestone near the end of his own journey.

'I am glad that you were in the country and will be able to make the funeral. She would have liked that.' He brushed an imaginary hair off the sleeve of his old black jacket. 'Will you be staying here?'

I hadn't even given it any thought. I looked around at the room I knew so well, part of a house that, to me, really was home. I considered for a moment. 'No, I think it's too soon. I must say goodbye to her, first. Perhaps, after a while, I could stay here again.'

He looked at me over his glasses as he put away some of the papers he'd apparently been reading while waiting for my arrival. 'Well, it's yours, so you'll be able to come back whenever you like.'

I hadn't even thought about her property, how she might have decided to dispose of it. 'Mine?' Even when I'd said that perhaps I could stay here again I hadn't thought of the consequences of the house's owner's passing, that perhaps already it belonged to someone else.

'The house and everything in it.'

I couldn't believe it. I stood there, seemingly locked in place, everything rushing past me, events happening at a speed incomprehensible.

'You are one of the two beneficiaries of her will.'

'Two? Only two?' I thought of Mother and Father; with me that made three.

'You and the University. Queen's.'

There were many people at the funeral, but, apart from Lacroix, no-one that I knew. A few came to me to offer condolences, apparently identifying me as the closest relative, but the majority came only to say private goodbyes to Grandmother, and departed after the service. There were no other family members at the cemetery, and a few that had followed the cortege stayed their distance from the grave. I thought of the funerals I had witnessed years before in Mexico - grief there was shared amongst all, and the departed went blessed into eternity. Grandmother had a dry, Anglo-Saxon leaving.

She had left instructions for an immediate burial. I thought it was because she had been separated from Grandfather for far too long, and wished to lose no time in joining him physically and spiritually. Perhaps, though, she'd weighed the odds of my being elsewhere and had seen no point in prolonging the interment. She'd had no reason to believe that Mother and Father would come.

Old Lacroix had timed it well, because he'd been at both the service and the cemetery, but there was an envelope, sealed under his signature, on the hall table when I returned to the house. When I opened it, there was a note in a different hand I knew so well, which said 'For you, Alastair. With my love.' On a ribbon taped to the letter was a key.

I wondered why Lacroix hadn't given it to me earlier, but, looking at the key and the words that went with it, I thought perhaps that this had been a special instruction, a particular gift to soften the leaving. Had I been out of the country it might have stayed in his possession for some time.

The key was one of those old brass ones that turn dull when unused. It took me back to Carlos and the massive locks on his *bodegas*, though it was much smaller than anything he would have used. I walked into the front room in which we had spent our evenings talking, and switched on the standard lamp behind the old wingback chair that had been Grandfather's. Pausing for a moment, I poured a glass of amber *fino* from a decanter on the sideboard, another taste Grandmother and I had acquired together, and then sat in the chair, looking at the other empty one in front of me.

The room itself was comfortable, with furniture of a marque simpler than the Victorian pieces commonly found in older Kingston. Grandmother, perhaps as a result of living with Grandfather and his spartan machinist's mind, liked elegant curves and lighter colours, so there was matching of beech with the paint on the door and hue of the carpet. I think most of it had been made to order, and, perhaps, proving the universality of his skill with a pencil, to Grandfather's design. I absorbed it all for a moment before looking down at the key in my hand.

I don't really think it was a mystery, though I had always found it curious that the bookcase was locked. It always had been, and Grandmother had never opened it in my presence, nor told me about it. I knew all the contents of the other two, because we'd discussed books as we'd discussed travel, and most were titles I'd suggested she read. My recommendations got little more than a nod or a shake when the next visit came around, no time to waste on what had already been read, what was the next on the list? She had the voracious appetite of one from a different age, who'd not had the education of a more modern woman, the one rejected by my mother, but who had come upon reading as a wonderful way to fill opening voids. I don't think there was a single one of my recommendations that she didn't read, and those two bookcases said that she'd also found some other things by herself.

And I'd assumed they were personal papers, kept behind glass in a way that made them a formal presence in a slightly less formal room.

There was little resistance in the tumblers, and just a quiet click of the whole mechanism as I turned the key. But it filled the room with sound, and it felt like a last word from the person, who, until I'd come through the front door today, had been closest to me for years.

Old notes. That was the first impression. Pages, folders, scrapbooks, all full of hand-written, pencilled notes. The second impression was that they must have been my grandfather's, because they were written in male hands. Slightly chauvinistic, perhaps, that thought, because I've seen many a bold female hand which I could not have ascribed to a woman had I not known the writer. However, there was something clearly male about the visual form of the letters and words. The third impression was that there was much that was older than my grandfather, because there were dates also. Early and mid 1800's.

I wondered why Grandmother hadn't left me something saying whose notes they were. But then I realized that I was looking for something as simple as a loose sheet of paper on top, saying, 'Dear Alastair, here are so-and-so's recollections of....'. Far too simple that, knowing her. If she hadn't mentioned them in life, perhaps she had had no intention of mentioning them near death, content to leave me a puzzle, perhaps keep me close to her that while longer.

There is something about a very old object which draws attention not given to something quite new. Packed away in a trunk I have a collection of a dozen small Sung dynasty brushwashers, small circular bowls with rich green or brown translucent Celadon glazes. Each bowl has two fish inscribed in the bottom, circling after each other. For such small bowls to invoke a sense of peace, of harmony in that endless chase, is the apex, perhaps, of art which disappeared with its founding culture, consumed by another. In my hands they warm me. I collected them during a different chapter of my life, on long hauls through small Asian backwaters, when they were still relatively cheap. They were manufactured in mainland China many hundreds of years ago, and traded throughout southeast Asia. Now, when they surface from their centuries-old resting places, sometimes the graves where they were meant to stay, they sell for a fortune. By their wear mine almost certainly had a less worrying provenance, and most carried small flaws, which made them a lot cheaper, even then. And every pair of fish is slightly different, which, apart from their colour, is the only possible root of personality in clay fired immobile.

The three books, in blue cloth cover and with faint gold tracing, were slim. Time had faded each one slightly differently, though they'd probably been identical when they were new. What their original intended purpose would have been I couldn't tell, because I thought it likely that bookbinders of the time only sold ready-bound volumes of paper marked for book-keeping. Though if the sheets in them were devoid of any manufacturer's mark, including columns, the tight earthworm curls of a very steady, black-ink, copperplate hand were as commanding as two, simple, eternal fish. The tops and tails of s's and t's flew away from the body of the line, but came back looping into the spires of l's, b's and d's, and the undercarriages of the y's, g's and q's. It was a pleasure just to watch the movement of the words across the page, a sight far more beautiful than their content. In my first encounter with that story, it seemed to me hideous.

The *fino*, and two more, were long gone. I dug an old steamer trunk of mine out of Grandmother's basement, filled it with the contents of my bookcase, and called a taxi. The driver blanched when he saw what was waiting on the doorstep, probably worried that his back would be the one paying the price of loading it into the cab, but I took an end and we managed to stow it without too much difficulty. I took a last look around the room before switching off the standard lamp. As the pool of light dissolved, street light filtered through the curtains, and from the dark shadows of the chairs I had a strong feeling of a double presence. It was as if I had acknowledged that they were together, where they wanted to be. I wondered if I'd ever be free of that feeling. The light outside beckoned, and I knew that I'd always find it difficult to return to this room in the dark.

It did not take long to install myself in one of the downtown hotels. But by the time I'd done so, my hunger was rumbling up from below, so I walked up Princess Street, found a small restaurant serving a menu sufficiently eclectic for a palate currently as depressed as mine. I'd only intended to be gone an hour, but half a litre of wine later, accompanied by some reasonably good pasta, I felt myself drawn into those three very old diaries , which absorbed me into a time well over a century ago.

The trunk sat untouched all night, the diaries enough to contemplate. But the next morning I emptied the contents of the trunk onto the other bed in my room. It took me most of the day to leaf through everything else more thoroughly than I had done the night before, and to leave it all in neat piles. I sorted it all by texture, colour, script, date, and any other variable that seemed important. The paper ran from the yellowed heavy parchment-like material that was the oldest, to a flimsier but still stiff stock of a hundred years later. But the youngest pile was still thirty years old, with what had turned out to be my grandfather's hand reasonably elegantly noting the results of his own research.

I thought about Grandmother and decided that she had given weight to the matter because Grandfather had, and that it was now in my hands because of that joint deliberation, even if the latter was an outcome of deaths ten years apart. And it was the original writing in the diaries themselves which had caught me, beginning as it had with that note of irreverence ..... ` *If there is one thing for which I can thank God, while He considers it necessary for me to remain in this hellhole, it is that my boots no longer smell of horse piss. Were it any different, I should indeed be suffering. As it is, I have only to put up with my thoughts. But He has given me time, so as it appears to be His wont, I shall use it profitably. Though where the profit is to me, I cannot see.'*

I had read this before coming to Grandfather's notes, thinking, at that point, that perhaps I had nothing more than just an old manuscript. Until that point I read it as some sort of background to a Georgian novel. But Grandfather's notes put paid to that idea, for his research gave the story credibility - not just to the content of the diaries but of the other papers also. So, understanding Grandfather, I also came to understand Grandmother, and knew that I should take the matter seriously. For it had been very serious to that original writer: *Believe my story or not, as you will. But understand this: that I may shortly be condemned to death. And if I am, then justice will not have been done, for I swear on my sister's grave, not that grave which has me encarcerated here, that I did not do it. So all I can do is present to you the facts in the hope that you may be a kindlier jury. Even if, by the time you deliberate, I am dead.*

But perhaps I'd had an inkling of it all while absorbed in that first *fino*, for there had always been an air of mystery about the past. Grandmother had been clear enough about the recent family tree, for she'd not wanted my own provenance hidden from me. But, even though she'd admitted to a great deal of personal knowledge about more distant ancestors, she had kept that knowledge to herself, changing the subject with a quiet murmur if ever it arose. I'd seen it as one of her few fancies, that there were other things perhaps less comfortable than me in our heritage, but she'd always disabused me of the notion if our conversation headed in that direction.. 'Different matters, Alastair, awkward, lost in time. One day....., but now, pour me a little more *fino*.'

Shilling

The panelling in the tall window bays was a rich dark red, blood red almost, and the sun kissed it before penetrating further into the room and falling on uncarpeted but painted boards. These floor boards were a mustard yellow. Motes hung on the air, dancing to whatever slight currents were made by the occupants as they moved to their various tasks.

'I should think,' said Mr Richard Cartwright, 'that the King will make a pretty profit.'

Cartwright sat at his large oak desk, writing. He was always writing, now and then pulling his penknife out of a fold of his clothing to readjust the tip of his quill. The room and all it contained were his, even the clerk because of his articles, though the young man before him, to whom Cartwright spoke as he wrote, could not be said to be a chattel.

The young man was there because of his father, a good friend to Cartwright above and beyond any necessity of trade, and between the two of them there had been a spoken agreement that the youth should learn how business may turn a profit. The youth conceived of himself as an apprentice to this business, and accepted his role as unpaid minion. He was at that stage when learning was suddenly appreciated as the gate to the future, rather than, as previously, a boring necessity which others forced upon one.

His father understood business as that larger element of trade beyond just buying something for a penny and selling it for two. He had no need to send his son to Cartwright to learn the latter. He was not a businessman himself, rather he was a martial man, but he had fought his battles almost thirty years before, and was now seen as a solid leading citizen who was able to live from both agriculture and justice. Farmer and magistrate would have been the technical terms. But he saw limits for his son in at least one of these professions, and considered commerce a better pathway to future, filial prosperity.

The young man now knew there was the King to deal with, merchants in Montreal, bateauxmen on the river, and whatever client might voice his needs uplake from Kingston. Trade, he had grown to understand, possessed dimensions of time and risk. At first he had also thought distance was important, but Cartwright saw it differently.

'No, young man. Distance is also time and risk - the greater the distance, the longer the time and the higher the risk. So, if you are able to gauge time, then will you know how to cost your freight. And remember, there are three risks - Man, King and God. The first you cope with by common sense and payment on delivery. The King, who believes he *is* God, is but a tax on everything you do, so equate him to so many percent of costs. To God, you pray that he put nothing in your path while dealing with Man and King, for those two are enough for any merchant.' He paused. 'But God determines your profit, and against Him you play the underwriters.'

The young man thought in truth Cartwright determined his own profit, for he kept a written record of all transactions, and knew almost to the penny how much he could get from God. He had been at it for twenty year, and of all in Kingston who would copy him, none could read the mood in Montreal as could he. But he professed to hate trade, suggesting that it were a demeaning livelihood. The young man thought, given that Cartwright accrued wealth faster than anyone he knew, that he dissembled when he said this.

But his comment on the King's profit spoke to something else. Engineering, the young man thought, if that be the word for something made to happen on a calculated basis. Though this were not directly the King's doing, for the War had been declared against him. But his minions, on what the citizens called *this benighted frontier*, were fighting it, and those who calculated that it would be thus stood to make a fortune from it. War, the young man was beginning to know, created demand. Merchants satisfied that demand. And sometimes, when the King's ships planned passage downriver or uplake, cargo space was offered at a fee. Whether that fee got *to* the King was another matter. But since all the King's Captains wore a magisterial label, and even if the monies were deposited no further than a trouser pocket, it were the King who was paid.

Beyond the doors of Cartwright's countinghouse, the town had the makings of a capital. Strategically placed for both trade and defence, and understood to be so, it was full of an early 19th century activity of the type considered the culmination of Man's ingenuity on establishing and holding a frontier. Both, trade and defence, or establishment and possession, required money. Money had to be made. But it could only be made by those who already had it. So the wealthy underwrote both commerce and war, and these, because of this very simplest of common denominators, were therefore nothing more than strategies to be played against each other. Notes were issued against a shipment of wheat or a regiment of foot, and as the latter consumed the former, *empire*, even of this very primitive kind in Upper Canada, was a highly profitable thing.

There may actually have been some British reluctance to funding ventures in Upper Canada. Europe was coming out of the Napoleonic War, and a Treasury which might have been considering a breathing space in order to put a nation's finances in order, would probably not have jumped at the chance to send men and ships perhaps ten times as far as it had had to send them over the preceding decade. So far it had managed to coast along on a very small contingent, a few able military men, a few thousand displaced loyalists, and would perhaps have been happy with a status quo. But America changed that, deciding that its nose had been ground into the sand of Europe's beaches once too often, beaches that it had not been permitted to touch during years of blockade, and that *its* wealth was suffering. Whether or not King George had come out of his madness, the irony of having to fight his lost colonies a second time could well have driven him straight back into it.

But perhaps something in the air affected Sir James Yeo, Commodore, just arrived to take command of His Majesty's Navy, on the lake. It were not, yet, much of a navy of which to take command, perhaps the *Royal George*, at 22 guns, its flagship, so to speak. And, until Commodore Yeo arrived, perhaps it were better called an army, for they called it the Provincial Marine, with the army at its helm.

Because of the depredations of the Americans on the water, the *Royal George* had to stay in Kingston harbour all winter of 1812. Captain Isaac Chauncey, come to take command at Sackets Harbor, controlled the lake once he had launched the 24 gun *Madison*.

All winter of 1812 were there ships under construction, at both Kingston and York, even though dear General Brock had considered it better to remove the naval yard from York to Kingston. Mr Richard, Colonel Cartwright, had thought him correct, the defence of two yards doubly difficult. But General Brock gave himself in battle almost immediately, and there was no-one equally able to argue the point with General Prevost.

Sir James arrived in Kingston with much fanfare, and, they say, as many as 450 seamen and 36 officers, and, one might be tempted further to say, the navy was born. But Chauncey pre-empted him, taking and burning the yards at York - though not without cost. The magazine was mined and blown by the British, killing a goodly number of Chauncey's force. Perhaps this action lost him his single chance to win the war at one blow, York instead of Kingston, because now Sir James was come, surely he would match Chauncey shot for shot?

The trouble began innocently. The young man sat again in front of Cartwright, who was expounding. `I have been here these twenty year, and built this business from the ground. My contacts and agents in Montreal were gained at personal effort and expense. Foster came in with all his continental wealth and thought that he could wrest much of this forwarding business from us,' Cartwright waved around him, indicating Kingston in general, `but he forgot the goodwill.' Cartwright had called this the war before the War, a spat, really, over trade. `I would not imply that he still poses any threat, but he still has his agent, Franck, looking for any opportunity. In all that you do on that side of the river, keep your ears open to mention of their names.'

Some might quibble at there being innocence in a time of war. These people were innocents, though, if they thought that war would burn itself out. It took flame on the Atlantic shore, and sent its sparks far across country to their lake.

The trouble began because Cartwright had wanted for intelligence. The young man's father smiled wryly at him when he said this. `I should never have thought it of you, Richard.'

Cartwright himself chuckled. `Not me in person. Us - you, me, the others. There is nothing simple about this war. Survival depends on our playing the game very closely, even as we satisfy the political ends forced upon us. It will be trade that keeps us strong. It will be trade that defines the value Brittania considers her colonies to represent. Let us say, even as I hope it, that there will be some sort of negotiated settlement once those American hotheads reconsider their foolishness. If Brittania recognizes that we are an increasing source of wealth, she will weigh her position very carefully; if we are a deadweight, she may just cut our cable at the hawsehole.'

`Do you not get intelligence from your customers, your clients?'

`I do. But much of it is hearsay, too passive. We need active knowledge - hot from the oven, so to speak.'

`How do you propose to gather it?'

`What would you say to a troop of scouts? Young men with energies to burn?' He glanced across the countinghouse to his friend's son.

` An official commission?' The youth's father was ever cautious as to unrecognizable initiatives (but eager for furtherance for his son).

` I think I could get Macdonnell to agree.'

` And what, really, would they do?'

` Tell us what these damned Americans are doing.'

` And what would we do with this ...... *intelligence*?'

` Seize the opportunities made.'

'A King's Border Scout? It has an interesting ring.'

Cartwright smiled. 'That will depend on Macdonnell.' Macdonnell would have to send to Prevost, in Montreal, to agree to commissions and a name. Both knew that Prevost never took such decisions instantly.

'What do you say, Cameron?' asked the young man's father.

'I think you are sending me into adventure,' said Cameron MacNeil. 'But two would be safer than one. Perhaps I should talk to Duncan.'

The father recognized the wisdom in his son's idea. Safety, on a frontier, was something asked of God, but Cameron's mother would see it differently. Duncan would be given the responsibility.

Cameron MacNeil loved history. Through its study he had learnt that the vicissitudes of war were many. He loved less that the common man bore the cost, so much cannon fodder at a shilling a day. Oh, not exactly, perhaps, but he knew that term, the King's shilling, was rife with irony and that one did not dare to suggest, on this far frontier, that a soul was worth a little more. The King would not condescend to listen.

He discussed war with his father, and knew that it was too easy to suggest that war was a face-to-face fight. His father pointed out that in Europe they had been fighting for years, shuttling from battlefield to battlefield, fertilizing the soil everywhere with so much blood. Harvest was never better than after a gory struggle. 'Only God knows how many lives it took for Wellington to drive Napoleon off his imperial heights and into exile,' the father said, adding 'though if I am honest, some army clerk in Whitehall probably has the exact figure.' He paused. 'Though again, if I think about it, Napoleon did fight face-to-face, never learning that his mighty columns were outdated in their frontal assaults against fluid, well-fought British squares.'

Cameron knew that could never be, here. They would have to clear the forests of Upper Canada to make the open spaces required for a pitched battle. Here, their small forts and blockhouses with their few acres of open land were but momentary defences - lack of food and ammunition would rapidly raise a siege against any of them.

So the common men and women of the settler colony of Upper Canada had been pitched against the settler colony of friends and relatives on the other side of the river (and lake). But, as Cameron had grown to understand it through Mr Richard's eyes, this were a single economy, no distinction made about from whom one bought or to whom one sold. And if either side were to survive, it was very important that this economy prosper. No-one wanted to fight, let alone win. So while the havoc was here, the `dogs' of war barked very distantly.

Insomnia

The dream comes often. Across the table from me is a woman's face I cannot see. I am telling her about Peru. We seem to be intimate, because I know her first name, though it never comes to me at any time then or afterwards. While I talk to her I see the Andes, the *puna*, and in particular three people.

'*Potato*,' I say. The woman thinks I am talking about an ingredient of the dish in front of her. '*Potato is a staple for them.*'

But flowing images compete with this apparent confession, images showing my guide, dressed in a maroon woollen jumper, and pants that have seen so much work they are a colour of their own. A multi-hued knitted helmet with ear flaps covers the hair, but the rest of the face is bare burnt sienna, around a nose found in Rome as well as among the Incas. His voice is soft: '*Descansa, señor*, rest. We cannot do this in one day, anyway. An hour more and we can find where to pass the night.'

The story seems to come out naturally, but in the dream I have no way of knowing what I speak and what I hear. I think I put most of it into words, but even if it is presented disjointedly to the woman she says nothing. I have no idea if she too can see the simultaneous Andean diorama.

Somehow I am unable to escape the need to state historical fact. '*Potato comes from the Peruvian Andes. The early Europeans took it back and spread it worldwide. But the Peruvians still eat it as they ate it then.*' I empty a soup dish and the main course comes. Apparently I've chosen quail, and the bird sits on a nest of vegetables, no potato in sight. The woman has chosen fish. I am drinking a lot of wine, knowing it will lubricate access to hidden places.

'*They make a gruel with the darkened flesh of the bitter potato.*' And I see it as it is, being shared with three people. The dish brims with it, and the minute curlicues of the cooked quinoa grain. I see that it is winter, but that the stew's ingredients are from last summer's harvest. It is the only food, my hosts say, what we eat every day. They smile their happiness on it. Quinoa is stored in sacks around them, but they dance, telling me that bitter potato must be dehydrated first. They show me how, with frost and feet, exposing the tubers during autumn nights to sharp freezing, and then treading them the following day when they thaw. Nights and days flash, showing the sun fueling the evaporative process. It takes several days, and the result is ugly. But their breath states that it is the staple at this altitude, the key to life. As I eat it, the taste becomes wonderful, belying foul colour.

` *They are very hospitable, caring even.*' And another image comes closer now, that day. Talk is quiet, in what my dream says is Quechua, glances including me, and I find that I understand the language. But once the meal is finished, my guide reverts to Spanish. 'Would you like to ask these people some questions, *señor?*'

Omnipotent vision takes in the high Andean stone-built communities, scattered houses amongst small, walled paddocks. Stone there is plenty of, though no mortar, and the wind comes in one wall and goes out the other. It is bearable during this early afternoon, but a thought of night brings a different sense: intense cold. The image enhances the cooking fire, which sends most of its smoke with the wind, ectoplasmic fingers escaping through the walls, but enough remains to sting my eyes. My hosts and guide seem enured to it, unaware of the outward flow, though they are gathered as if the warmth given by the small flames is important.

Between me and my dream woman my quail sits untouched, incubating whatever sits under it in its nest.

In the stone hut the other woman clears away dirty plates, and stokes the fire. The husband looks expectantly at me. *'Por favor, señor.'*

To my dream woman I say: ` *I wanted to talk about the Espada Dorada, but because such a direct question would be considered rude we talk about the weather and the promise of next year's crops. His family was well, he thanked Dios, so he had little to complain about. I asked about security.'*

'And security? Do you have much trouble here?' Halfway to where the *Espada* were known to have visited, and done much more, could not be expected to be safe.

I tell her: ` *He gave me the traditional answer of any peasant living on the edge of violence.'*

'Our safety is in God's hands, *señor*, and in Him we trust' '. He makes the sign of the cross but with a glance toward a mountain top, and I see the shadow of a completely different and far more ancient deity. I catch his unspoken thought: We do not expect much of the military.

Again I say to her: '*And I went on digging. "Do you often receive visitors?" His wife, seated on a stool beside the fire, span wool on a drop spindle, but, on hearing my question she also made the sign of the cross. She dropped the spindle and it fell directly into the fire. She covered her mouth with a hand as she gasped, and looked at me in horror. "El trae la muerte, tambien." He brings death, too.*'

The man apologises and says that sometimes his wife thinks she sees things. He tells me to forget what she said. But he goes on. "Which ones, *señor*?" he asks. "There are those on the move in the night, whom we pray will leave us alone, and there are those who come in the day and take what they want, in the name of the law. Against that, we pray just as much. If God wishes, he will continue to bless our fortune. Neither one is for poor people. Generally, they bring death."

I tell her: '*And I understand that his wife has foreseen his response.*'

'*But why did she say that of you?*' My dream guest's plate shows its underlying pattern, spiralling silver threads competing with the swirl of sauce pushed in the opposite direction. I am looking at it because I can't see her face, perhaps don't want to know who she is.

'*At the time I thought it was just the fear of an outsider, an unknown bringing unknown consequences.*' But in him, too, I see the same fear as in his wife, though he hides it better.

In the afternoon I walk with them both to an assembly point, a place where the community comes to talk. I hear and see them discuss matters essential to high-altitude survival, crop rotation patterns, communal grazing rights, tithes for land conservation activities paid for in labour. I do not consider these strange matters for a dream, not knowing that this is what it is. At the end, he brings some neighbours to where I sit, and we spend an instant or an hour recounting what had happened and to whom. Murder and rape are the commonest results of an unexpected call, day or night.

The quail is gone, swallowed untasted somewhere in that discourse, and the remaining vegetables appear coarse-textured, unappetising. I am aware of anger and I eat them to cool it. I am brought memories of the smooth face of his wife, unprotesting at the life thrust upon her, but finally torn into anguish at what the last few moments of her life brings. They make her husband watch, to be sure that he feels no sense of victory, cannot slip off into death without having begged for something. To me they decide to give not quite all of that, adding the denial of oblivion, for death ends the lesson for him to whom it is being taught, and they want to be quite sure that I remember it for ever.

Each time I wake, shouting and shivering.

I've stayed in a thousand hotel rooms, each a box to keep me penned for a while. There is no allure or luxury to a hotel. The tricks architects play to foster the illusion of innovation and originality very rapidly pall, often defeated by the designer who followed behind and filled the space with other boxes.. The only way I know of lessening the boredom is to abstract myself from the physical surroundings and bury myself completely in my writing. So, often, I would write to survive the pressure of those depressing walls, leaving the bounds of the brick that hemmed me in, through whatever gateway my subconscious presented. The journalist in me was only a part; there were always other words, written, and then locked away.

And it appeared that Grandmother had locked away words from an almost identical spirit. Something in his words caught a part of my mind, and I saw him in his cell suffering the burden of the walls on top of everything else for which he had been blamed.

Even though we all have ancestors from a number of generations that approaches the infinite, I make the common assumption that they lived and died without direct effect on me and mine. I found the statement: *I am a common man, victim of a common plot.* But if he had died for it, had there not to be some consequence that was making itself felt today? I am no less guilty than any other in believing that the effects of today on our lives must be so much more important than events of two hundred years ago. Yet they must have felt the same. And if he hadn't died, what would have been the consequence? And, yes, he *was* my ancestor. Had he lived, would it just have meant more cousins?

So my current hotel room became my channel into his life, his writing so stark I could smell the smell that to him was absent.

Blessed be God that He has, until this day, given me health, a fine wife, and one child. Were I less cognizant of this fortune, I might complain the more, but no man should misconstrue what is already good in complaints about a bitter present

Cameron MacNeil, a King's Border Scout, though in truth my family is far from the border that gives me my name, and the King's Border is the one just beyond my cell window, below which I can hear the sound of the river trade. My wife would be better off far from here, as I may not see her again until we come together under the Lord.

On these facts I will not dwell. I wish only to present to you my case, which I will base on the facts that I know, and the others they are using against me. Here I stand in my own defence, though the court has given me a lawyer. He, I fear, is more concerned for his wig.

But it is this great lake that lies just to the west, and how Man (or King and Congress) decided to use it in this struggle, that has me here, that and Messrs Yeo and Chauncey, Commodores both, Heads of their respective Navies, and mad for the biggest ship you ever saw. For they began a race, considering that absolute domination of those waters was the key to absolute victory in everything else. They are racing still.

I came out from within his walls with a sense of surprise, for I suddenly understood that this had happened no more than half a mile away in the founding days of the city - the date of the Court Martial confirmed it. But my surprise related more to what we see today as the visible elements of the military history, for it was easy to believe that the massive stone walls of Fort Henry were what had incarcerated Cameron MacNeil - they have the look of Ages. But the truth is that he was dead almost before the Fort was begun, and that he must have been held in a much simpler stockade. In fact, the city around it would barely have been started, and the eventual hordes of stonecutters that must have worked the quarries to deliver so much ashlar would still have been small teams of local masons.

Kingston is a city that tells you it has some sort of history, but it is all wrapped up in those gray limestone walls. The first immigrant settlers have slipped into the past, not even a distant past, but into a history which, perhaps, while caring for them, does not necessarily place them in the correct context. Military acts are re-enacted constantly at the Fort, but most of the relevant, local, military history was over by the time it was built, so it is a false backdrop to Lieutenant Cameron MacNeil. Lieutenant he had been, but tenant of a place no longer to be found.

Walls take your mind, and square them as a room is square, and it was no more than a small step into another room, four other walls, but still military walls. *Generalísimo* Pablo López Martín was within them, as was a different sense of death, and for a moment I stayed swimming between two worlds, neither one the present, but feeling my connection to both. And in that moment came knowledge that I was to understand what led Cameron MacNeil towards death as well as I was to understand what had similarly led me.

Then I went straight back into that old prose, beautiful in its visual elegance, solid but bare in its march towards fate. *If it were a race, then to have held them as we did, keel by keel, mast by mast, was a feat almost no man of us expected. Because Chauncey has his men to hand, men who start at the tree and make a ship from its root in forty days. Yeo is at the mercy of the King, every knee, bolt and trunnion bought at his whim, to build ships that His Lords of the Admiralty decide are what should be built; but before they are, much of the ironware for each one has to be transported across thousands of miles of ocean, up river, and through the last treacherous waters into the calm bay at our feet. There, we put form to what they send.*

I wondered if Cameron had spoken with a Scots accent. Though he would have been born in the New World, he would still have been surrounded by native Scots men and women, most of whom, because of the regimental settlement patterns, would still have been his neighbours. And as many of the rest would have been Irish, the daily presence of Gaelic would have maintained old ways, pronunciation among them. So, right or wrong, his words spoke to me this way, as he took me through the whole story.

At first I misunderstood the `*root*'; but another reason made me look at some of the other papers, and I came to understand that he referred not to the root of the tree, but the fact that Chauncey could bring shipwrights from the Atlantic seaboard, the latter suffering from a blockade constructed from the Napoleonic conflict, and fashion all his needs on the spot. His were the native designs, true New World warships; Yeo's were the Imperial wolves of the world's oceans, ships so recently tried at Trafalgar, and in which the Empire's trust rested, so no need to fashion anything different. *Though truly they are little different, for in the end they will carry an hundred guns, for that is at the root of the madness, all for control of this Lake.*

It was not a long war - started in 1812, it was over by 1815. But it was as significant as the war that brought the colonists independence, because the Americans lost it.

Queen's

Grandmother and I had not often walked through the University campus, though it lay not far from her house; we had preferred the river. Lacroix's call took me there unexpectedly, 'You'll remember I told you that the University was the other beneficiary? Well, it wishes to honour your grandmother. Will you go to the unveiling to say a few words?'

'Unveiling?'

'Yes.' And said no more.

'When?'

Lacroix was consistently brief: 'Tomorrow, 4pm. Can you make it?'

'Yes. But where should I go?'

'Find the Faculty of Engineering; Dean's Office.'

'Will you be there?'

'No. Goodbye, Mr MacNeil.'

'What are they unveiling?'

But he had already hung up.

Queen's is a university with elements common to Fort Henry: extensive use of limestone, annual ceremonial re-enactments, colours fluttering martially at the flagstaff. The abstract glances given by the older passers-by suggest that they are present in different historical time. I found the Dean's Office by consulting the campus map.

`Well. A pleasure to meet you, Mr MacNeil.' He was a slightly untidy man, but warm with his courtesy. `Speech prepared?' Other things were still demanding his attention, and he said it in a way that indicated that I knew what I was there to do.

`I'm afraid you'll have to tell me what I should be ready for. I can't speak to anything if I don't know the details.'

He showed some surprise. `Old Lacroix didn't tell you? Alright, then. How about the MacNeil Endowment Fund for Post-Doctoral Studies in Mechanical Engineering?'

There are times when you understand that you have passed a period mired in some sort of fog. I cast my mind back to the formalities of the funeral and realized that there had not been any formal reading of the will. I was not named an executor, perhaps to appease Mother and Father. I had been informed by Lacroix of the deeding of the house. Until he'd mentioned the University I'd made no assumptions of other property being willed except for that fleeting thought that, in her generosity, Grandmother had probably made some sort of financial bequest to her distant children. She'd lived simply, and I'd not thought her rich. 'How much did she leave to the University?'

`More or less, a million.'

It was obvious that my grandfather's success had netted more than just a reputation. He'd been brilliant at what he did in a time when industrial processes were becoming rapidly and progressively more sophisticated. A pre-electronic age, perhaps, but that made his skills even more needed, because industry on the whole was no slouch, and there was no such thing as standing still. He had honed processes to the point where it would take the quantum leap of electronics to open the field to a brand new game. My thoughts took me inside, back to Grandmother, and the house, and I must have appeared lost there. The Dean moved some papers on his desk and brought me out of times past. `There were some things she didn't tell me.' But I was sure Mother knew, and was furious that it hadn't been put into her hands.

`Time to tell us what you do know. That's what we'd like. Some colour.'

So colour I gave them, a lecture-hall full of academics and students, administrators and local press. Among them, I found out after, was a couple of representatives of the very industry that my grandfather kept in business, humming along on his genius. I told them all of my grandmother and the meaning that her house held for me. I told them that I never knew my grandfather beyond his pipesmoke and bony knee, so was unable to talk to what had been the focus of the endowment. But I told them that Grandmother valued, above and beyond all else, where knowledge took you, what it made you, what it gave you. And then what you gave back. And I told them that I missed her, and was thankful that there would always be something at Queen's which would remind others of both her's and Grandfather's existence. They applauded me politely. The Dean hauled me off to the reception afterwards, once the industry types had given me their business cards.

`Great talk, Alastair. May I call you Alastair? Good. Yes, great talk. Must have been great to have grandparents like that.'

I thought he'd probably not heard more than a superficial message, but he was intent on cordiality and did it in his way. I was the human image of the generosity Grandmother had shown. That image had to be watered and petted for a few minutes more.

`Think we can add five Post-docs to the department. Assuming we can get ten percent on it, of course. Great at a time like this. Money's scarce, you know. Have to prise it out of industry. Government's not giving. Up to the private sector. Hard to do research without money. Great grandparents you had, Alastair. Lucky man.'

It appeared that some of his Faculty's members had raced for the reception faster than he'd dragged me there, or else had decided to forego the pleasure of listening to me, because there was a welcoming line waiting beyond the door. Half a dozen faces, old and young, some of the staff who would get to share in the endowment as supervising professors.

`Hi, Jack Gratton, how are you.'

`Mr MacNeil, so pleased to meet you. Nancy Wemblay.'

`Steve Laroux.'

`Gord Knutts. Sorry about your grandmother.'

`Yes, tragic. Welcome. I'm Jeff McCartney, by the way.'

`Didn't follow in the old man's footsteps, eh, Mr MacNeil? Happens, you know. Fred Webster.'

Hands from soft to hard, but not the hands of a craftsman like my grandfather. Hands of academics, hands like journalists. Their touch stayed with me a lot longer than any of the names, the journalist in me clearly off-duty. The Dean brought me the scotch and water I'd asked for, and the door squad, its immediate duty over, dispersed for its own rations before gathering around again. Attending the Dean more than me. Faces started to sink in, paler than mine, desk-bound bodies with mostly short hair, except the woman. Nancy something? All showing what probably went for excitement over the bequest, and how it would invigorate the Faculty, their Departments.

`Not often someone is so generous.' A kind face on a lean body.

45

`Right, Gord. Endowment Funds have to be big these days to bring in the investment revenue even for a single position. Five! Well, we never expected it.' The only one there who looked even close to being an engineer, weathered face on stocky shoulders, the one with the hardest hands.

`Fred's so right, Mr MacNeil. Some other Faculties have had single endowments, which keeps them happy. But this means tremendous things for us. So much we can do. It's an electronic age, you know. But mechanical engineering is still the core of industry. Look at robots.' Long hair around a pale nervous face, but a body that had more woman in it.

`I must admit that I thought robots were much more electronic than they were mechanical.'

`Oh, yes. My goodness! Controls have to be, of course. But you must still have precision mechanics. It's the interface, Mr MacNeil. So exciting! The interface.'

The interface seemed to be of less interest to the others, who had started to glance into their glasses, or at the Dean.

`Mr MacNeil. Do you live in Kingston?' The pale face was more intense, though the eyes were distant, almost as if she'd forced them to be.

`I'm staying here a while, though I don't expect to be around permanently.'

`I think it would be a good idea if we adopted you.'

`I'm not sure I understand.' But there was suddenly an undercurrent, suggesting that the others did and that they were not in full agreement.

She looked playfully at the Dean. `You know what I mean; remember those sponsors?'

The Dean looked edgy, perhaps not liking the direction he was being pushed in.
`Catling Inc? Bracehams? Well...'

`Mr MacNeil.' Her gaze was back, more focussed, calculating. `We have been trying to get some money for a lecture series. Invited guests; you know. Perhaps if you were to bat for us, it would be more forthcoming. Play on your grandparents' legacy.'

`What Nancy means is that she has some partial commitments from these firms to support us. We haven't been able to get them to commit fully.' The Dean still looked edgy, but he clearly saw some advantage to Nancy's suggestion.

`You want me as a canvasser? Call them up, push them along?' It sounded the worst possible idea, and one that I'd run a mile from.

'Oh yes.' Nancy gushed. 'Thank you, that would be wonderful.'

'Wait a minute...'

'Nancy, I think Mr MacNeil needs to think about it. Perhaps he'd need to understand better what we're aiming for.' The Dean was uncomfortable now. The others seemed to have drawn into a tighter ring, some indefinable threat in the air.

'Oh.' She looked instantly crestfallen. 'Well, I'll leave it in your hands then. Perhaps you'll let me know.'

I had a feeling of having been backed into a corner, one I wanted to be nowhere near. 'I'm afraid it's unlikely I can help.' But somehow I had to decline gracefully. 'Perhaps, Dean, I can call you in a couple of days?' Communication via an official channel would probably be important.

'Of course, Alastair.' The Dean appeared equally relieved to have found a graceful way out, but he hadn't entirely discounted the idea. 'Any help you can give......., you know.'

A touch on my arm made me turn, and I found a different face: older, calmer, slightly familiar. 'Mr MacNeil, David Wranger. I heard your talk and enjoyed your description of your grandmother. She was a fine woman.' He was as tall as me, but perhaps the slight stoop would made him taller. Casual clothes that weren't cheap, and clear eyes looking through spectacles that sparkled in the lights.

'You knew her?'

He smiled at my loss of memory. 'We met at the funeral service.' Then he looked around and selectively took in the older faces. 'Most of us did, didn't we Fred?'

Fred Webster nodded. 'Dave is perhaps the odd man out here, Alastair. Not an engineer. So his was more of a social acquaintance.'

'Nothing wrong in those, Fred. Mary had many. But,' and he appeared unwilling for Fred or the Dean to continue the conversation, 'perhaps Mr MacNeil would like to relax.' He gaze was direct. 'Could I interest you in some dinner?'

The Dean thought this a good idea. 'Of course, David. Please take him. Lucky to have you looking after him. Mr MacNeil, thanks again for a great talk. Your grandmother'd be proud of you. Must have been great to have grandparents like that. Come by any time, and we'll introduce you to the new Post-docs. Give us a couple of months to find them, though.' A returning joviality wasn't fully mirrored in the group around him, which seemed as tense as it had during the previous conversation. Perhaps, at times, they found him as tiring as I did, though the hands were warmer this time, more assured. And, as we moved away, faces nodded amiably, but looked around to see who else was there, to join up with once the guest had gone - a University closing in on itself.

`Thank you for the invitation.'

Wranger smiled. `I saw it more as a rescue. They're not really your type.'

`My type?'

`May I call you Alastair? You're not an academic, Alastair. Anyone who heard your presentation knows that. You're a person who cares for people, who feels injustices. You were just treated to the warmest welcome engineers could possibly give you. But only because you're attached to the money. That's what they live for, what they breathe for. They weren't interested in you. You completed the formalities, that's all.'

I was surprised at his criticism. But I knew the truth in his argument - I'd thought it myself. It was because of Grandmother that I was here - I was her proxy. And there had been no reason for them to focus on anything other than the money, and ideas to get more. `But Fred implied that you are also an academic.'

He laughed. `That's fair enough. But I'm an historian, or was, anyway. Retired, now. And perhaps more interested in people than when I was working.'

`And you knew Grandmother well?'

`She and Mary were great friends. Occasionally we would have her to dinner - we enjoyed mixing Faculties. A dining table surrounded by historians is a deadly dull place.' There was a note of humour in his voice.

`But neither she nor Grandfather *was* Faculty.'

`He was in an honorary sense. Often I think that has greater validity than salaried appointments. They both gave much to the University.'

`I'm just learning how much.'

Wranger smiled. `Yes. Many people are.'

We didn't talk much in the drive from the University, which only took about five minutes. He was pensive, slightly distant, and I wondered whether he was regretting the invitation.

He pulled into a driveway beside a house not very different in age from Grandmother's, though only two storey's to Grandmother's two and a half. Foursquare, with a formal garden both in front and down one side. I could see evening light on the river beyond it.

We'd only just opened the car doors when a small blond-haired body hurtled out though a crack of light, and straight into his arms. 'Hi, Granpa. You're late.'

'Hi, pet. No, not really.' He smiled across at me. 'Say hello to Alastair.'

The little face didn't hesitate. 'Hello, Aster. Granpa, I'm hungry. Can we have dinner now? I've already got my PJs on, so I can stay up late and watch TV.'

Bathed, too, I thought. So it would be a family dinner, six of us.

'Any brothers and sisters?'

David shook his head. 'No, just little Penny.'

But little Penny had an ear for adult conversation, especially when the topic came close to her. 'Mommy's promised me a brother or a sister soon. She said she has to decide on a birthday, first. When she knows, she says I'll know.'

It sounded like a topic of frequent conversation, and I had a sense of an open family, frequent communication among them all.

'Come on now. I think Alastair needs a drink. And Granpa wants one too.' And little Penny shot out of his arms back through the shaft of light. He watched her go. 'Makes everything else worthwhile.' Then to me, 'Sorry. Come and meet the rest of the family, and then we can have dinner.'

I followed him through the open door.

Grandmother's staircase had gone up one wall. Here, the staircase was centre plan, right in front of me, with doors leading off to either side at its foot. A small landing disappeared to each side at its head. Lights seemed on everywhere, warmth on every wall, and the house spoke its friendliness to me, as straightforward as the Georgian period in which it was built. I followed David to the right, to what was evidently the reception room, parlour they might have called it then, a room of armchairs, sidetables, sideboard and paintings. The drinks were where one would expect them to be, on the sideboard, and a woman was right in front of it, clinking glasses.

'Hello, pet. A long day.' He walked across and kissed her cheek. 'This is Alastair. Alastair, Angela.'

I took a cool hand and saw an attractive woman in her thirties, casually dressed, though the blouse and charcoal-dark trousers carried more than a hint of formality. Only a coloured scarf at the neck softened the severity. But if the hand was cool, the smile was warm. `We have heard of you.'

David had mildly surprised me by confessing his acquaintance with Grandmother, but I hadn't expected it of his daughter. David laughed at my quizzical look. `You will be thinking that there is a motive for inviting you. Don't worry - this is purely social. I thought, when I heard you speak, that you looked tired and could do with a good meal.'

The lamplight was kind to him, reducing the fatigue that had also been evident in his face on our drive home, but he carried sadness. No wife, I thought. Mary's gone. He's living with his children.

The drinks came, three only, and we sat in chairs that wanted you in them, and I began to realize that, for the moment at least, we were only three. And then I wondered if it was the other way around, the old house, Grandmother, a young family's salary, and that perhaps Angela and her husband were living with her father.

`You knew Grandmother also?' I asked Angela.

`Really only after your grandfather died. She kept herself circulating. Trying not to slip into oblivion, I think.'

`I never had any idea. When I stayed with her, we spent most of our time alone together. Any walks were always down by the river. The campus stayed out of it. Something to do with my mother, I had thought. She'd always hated the place.'

`Your visits were when she disappeared from sight. When she reappeared she would apologize, but not say very much. Just that you had been in town.' She paused. `But I didn't see much of her for quite a while. Only when we moved in with Dad.'

There was silence, broken only when David stood up, and took all three glasses for a refill. But before he had a chance to redistribute them, Penny came haring through the door, and straight onto her mother's lap. `Dinner. I want dinner, Mommy. Now.'

`Then I think we'll take the wine with us,' David said.

Dinner had been perfuming the house since we'd arrived. Lamb, probably roasted. Penny climbed down and came over to me. `Here. I'll show you the way, Aster. Funny name you've got.' And she took my hand in hers for the walk back past the stairway, to the dining room opposite.

I think it had been a long time since I'd had a meal that satisfied all my senses. We remained three at dinner, well, three and a half, and there was no mention of a fourth. The lamb came with a vegetable I thought most children hated, but Penny devoured her brussel sprouts, two of them, with as much gusto as her roast potato. `Baa lamb, this,' she said, at one point. `Silly animals, to get eaten.' That seemed to finish the topic, in her mind anyway. She had the harmless precociousness of her age - something, in that quiet but close relationship with mother and grandfather that I thought would disappear when it was time for it to do so.

I spent most of the dinner listening to Angela talk to David about University affairs in general. She was clearly a Kingstonian, and seemed to me to be someone with a destiny in higher level civic affairs. I was surprised when she switched to her afternoon at work and revealed herself to be a policewoman. It had not been a good day, though probably because of Penny she went into little detail.

`We've had a spate of beatings, so I've spent a lot of time this week helping the victims through enquiries and identification lines. I've only just come out of one.'

`Unpleasant stuff.' And far too close to ground I'd recently trodden.

`Always.'

I saw her then as the public servant she probably was, old enough to be wise to the dirty ways of the world, but considerate to those who had suffered as victims. It helped to be a mother, I thought, both for the understanding it brought and the break it gave.

`Where has your travel taken you recently?' Dinner was over, and David gave me the question as he gave me my coffee.

`Peru, mainly. Occasional visits to its neighbours.'

`We see fascinating images of it. I expect the reality is quite different.'

`Grinding poverty in the main. Selling culture to tourism does little to ameliorate it.'

`What's your interest?'

`Terrorism and its roots. Why the poor suffer more as victims than the rich.'

`At high cost to life.'

`Life is cheap anywhere in the Third World, David. A peasant is a peasant, a chattel if he's not free. There are so many of them, that another springs into the place vacated by death. Animals are worth more.'

'What made you choose Peru?'

I'd often wondered the answer to that myself. 'Wanting to see the disparity between the European overlay and the original culture, I think. That is the root of it all. But the division is not as clear, perhaps. Five centuries is a long time, and distinctions have blurred. And had Europe not arrived, the original elite might have continued with policies that brought the same end - an exploiting upper class, mirrored by a military, which is not willing to make any concessions towards diminishing the disparity between those that have, and those that never have had.'

'Despite all the rhetoric?'

'Despite the rhetoric. Latin America talks a great deal, but the basic problems remain. It's all to do with power.'

'Aren't you in danger when you go there?' Angela had other thoughts in her mind. Perhaps a policewoman's.

The instant we began on Peru I knew there was a high probability that the conversation would take uncomfortable turns towards areas I could not yet deal with. But it would have seemed ungracious to change the subject completely, so I relied on the mind remaining numb, with little chance of a giveaway. 'There are different sorts of danger. I've come to work on the principal that if you are to meet your Maker then it is likely to happen anywhere. If you make a different assumption, then you get very little done. But, is it dangerous? Yes. There's a higher probability of an earlier and more direct route to the Maker in Peru than there is here. But it's more likely to happen on the streets of Lima than in the heights of the Andes.'

'Except you go looking for where it happens in the Andes.'

'Where it has happened. It doesn't necessarily strike in the same place twice.' That had been my working hypothesis. Three deaths proved it the poor one it had always been.

'You must speak Spanish.'

'I chose to live in Mexico for a few years.'

'Journalism again?'

'I wanted to write some articles about the US and its approach to its neighbours, especially its poorer southern one. To do that you have to live there. It was a contrast to Canada.'

'I remember.' David came back to life. '*Can't live without them*. I thought it was an interesting series.'

'I was quite a bit younger then. More ideals, too. Thought I could make people sit up and take note. But, again, it's a story of exploitation.'

'No such ideals now, Alastair? That's not what I read.' Angela was shaking her head.

'Different ones, perhaps. More personal ones. People as individuals, not pawns of economies.'

'Though your Peruvians are just that.'

'I can't do very much about that. But perhaps I can expose the bits that matter the most. And I think terror has to be very high on that list.' But now we were getting to where I definitely did not want to tread. Not that I saw it particularly as a subject not for postprandial discussion, but because I had no trust at all in my subconscious, and the possibility of a savage shaft of self-pity puncturing my very thin shell of survival. Oh, I used to write about it, and put all my feelings into words to be read. Now I had lost those feelings. And, before, if I did discuss it at a table, I did not do so casually, as if it did not matter. Once you have met it, it can never not matter. But I had never really met it, until this time.

'I think,' said Angela, as if she'd read my mind, 'I'll put Penny to bed. Storytime.' She got up in that natural way that stretches fabric onto a woman's body in ways which the touch of hands never seem to copy. Penny had stayed curled in her arms the whole time we'd been talking, and clearly was not far from sleep.

I moved, too, taking it as a signal that dinner was over, and that it was time to go.

'No. Stay a few minutes longer. Dad enjoys sharing his brandy, and then I'll run you back to your hotel. I won't be long.' She carried Penny out, and I listened to their slow progression up that staircase, quiet murmurs of secrets shared between mother and child.

We migrated back to the chairs that wanted you in them, and the brandy came. David was quiet a moment, but had that look all older people have when they want to say something and feel that formulating the words requires care. Or else he was just enjoying his brandy in a companionable silence.

'Are you going away soon?'

It was an odd question, but I didn't think it was meant unkindly.

'Not immediately. Not to Peru, at least.'

'Then I hope we'll see more of you.'

He got up and hunted through a pile of recordings, putting on an oboe selection that filled the room with melody that moved from angst-ridden to angelic. It was a poetic choice, though dangerous for me, undercurrents of my own sorrow swirling somewhere near my diaphragm. Angela, coming in well before it was over, quietly poured herself something and joined us without a word. This suggested that music was a language used in this house; such moments should never be hurried to their end even when they are disturbing.

But it did end, and it was finally time to go.

David's hand was as dry as it had been when we first met. 'Goodbye, Alastair. If you need some historical insights, call me.' It was another odd comment, but I was tired and it passed over my head almost without notice.

Angela was quiet in the car, and I had no reason to pursue a conversation, enjoying instead the presence of a woman. We were almost at my hotel before we broke the silence, and it was me who asked the question.

'Did your mother die long ago?'

She drove under the entranceway, and pulled up in front of the doors, turning the engine off before answering - that in itself a guide to the feelings the question engendered. 'Three years. Dad has been heartbroken ever since.' Then, a slight smile and an offered hand. 'Goodnight, Alastair. Thank you for coming. I hope we didn't pump you too much.' Then the engine was started up and a gear selected.

But, before I'd closed the door and ended an evening, there was one more piece of news.

'Penny says she likes you.'

In his notes, Grandfather said: *If there were anything that I wished, it was that Cameron knew that he did not lose the war.*

Till this point I'd focused on Cameron alone, wanting to know him, to understand him, and perhaps pull the single thread out of his story that would tell me what I felt, more and more, that he was trying to tell: this is who they *should* have hanged. But there were reams of other papers, too, and after my first sorting they'd sat on the second bed, catching my eye now and then, though not intruding into my singular line of thought. Though that was not truly accurate, either, for the dream intruded often. Sleep took a long time coming afterwards, and only by turning my thoughts towards Cameron could

I gradually relax. So I thought about his walls, rather than the many shades of mine.

But those other papers gradually called, more and more, and so a moment came when I put Cameron's book in its pile with the other two, and picked up a different hand in modern ink. And if I understood anything in that moment, it was that I would come to know a family that, before, had not stretched back beyond my grandmother.

I think my grandfather had constantly dreamt cams and bearings, because his notes were written in, round and over diagrams of all sorts. At the beginning I'd wondered whether there were some valuable engineering drawings in that bookcase, for there was much in Grandfather's hand. I say ʻhand', because that is how I saw each one, separate hands that were taking me back a hundred and seventy five years, shaking mine, welcoming me to the family. Through Grandfather's wish that Cameron had known that he'd not died on the losing side, I was coming to know more about that which he had also considered, and was beginning to understand his frustrations in not coming any closer to the truth.

Was it true that the Americans lost? It took me into areas that I'd forgotten about, though if anything is clear it is that the northern side of Lake Ontario is (still) in Canadian hands today. So Grandfather's analysis of what started the war, the price paid on both sides, and, eventually, the terms of settlement reached, convinced me that he was right. The ex-colonists started it, with territorial gain in mind, and ended up, on the eastern side of the continent, with what they'd had at the start. If anything, it forced people to draw lines on maps, setting in history those decisions on outcome. Had they been smarter they'd have bottled us up through trade. But it was still a period ruled by musket and cannon, and, if alliances were cared for, our first nations against their first nations. For, said Grandfather, if there was anything that really scared the Americans, it was the relatively greater success the British had in using native warriors in battle. But the Americans lost principally by failing to take Quebec right at the start. Then they had no way of stopping the men and supplies upon which Upper Canada depended.

Other wars, other struggles. *Hay que entender*, had said Carlos, you must understand that most of them are from similar communities, pushed into a desperate struggle because they see it as the only way out of poverty. Their allegiance is to an ideal, and even if it has Marxist roots, it would very rapidly lose those roots if they were to seize power. The intellectuals that goad them on would see to that. Who funds them? Anyone interested in destabilization, so who knows? But really they depend on themselves, and anything that they can squeeze from the countryside through terror.

Terror, a universal weapon; death, the universal ending. One struggle was little different from the other, fought on the backs of the masses, and generally keeping the elite safe. Only occasionally was there a commander who would take risk, such as Brock had taken and immediately paid for in 1812; *Generalísimo* Pablo would not stray from his barracks without knowing that there was not a single rifle or landmine threatening him for fifty kilometres. Some American commanders between 1812 and 1815 had shown similar fears.

But what fascinated Grandfather was the engineering aspect of the race, especially the escalation in size. Cameron put it differently: *We put too many eggs in a few large baskets. If Chauncey has learnt anything, after York, it should be that he can take a city with more, smaller ships, and if he loses one, then there are still others to bring his men home.* It was finding the balance between transport and firepower, thought Grandfather, though there was a real fear of the Royal Navy. But the Loyalists had given the Americans so many opportunities Grandfather had found it hard to understand why the Loyalists hadn't been wiped out. The Americans had been incapable of translating the strategy of small, onshore conflicts into nautical terms. The best opportunity was the Loyalist disaster they hanged poor Cameron for, but Chauncey stayed at home and went on building that ridiculous three-decker; as did Yeo.

From Grandfather's notes and the Court Martial record I knew that they'd gaoled Cameron soon after Popham's ill-advised foray into Sandy Creek, just southwest of Sackets Harbor, believing that Cameron had told Chauncey that Popham was coming. Yeo lost most of his seasoned sailors and marines, killed or captured, on that southeastern shore of Lake Ontario in a single day: May 30, 1814.

Iron

While Cameron thought they had intelligence of the first order, it seemed that there was already wind of the enterprise at Glasgie. Mr Richard had passed the news down to Macdonell at Prescott, who then sent for the pair himself. 'He asks me whether iron may be more profitable than potash,' said Mr Richard as he gave them their orders. 'You may tell him that at the moment I prefer the latter, though it would do little to win a war for him.'

It took a full day of hard riding to reach Prescott, and they approached the fortifications with some care. Evening was the favourite time for marauders from across the river, and they wished little to be mistaken for a pair of horse thieves. The sentry recognized an official letter, even if he was unable to read the name of its intended recipient, and directed them to the officer of the watch with only a little hesitation. 'You don't look like bloody Yanks and you're too dry to have swum the river.' He ignored the fact that they were mounted, and that the horses showed the stains of long-distance travel. 'Move on through there,' and he gestured with his chin, yelling almost immediately, 'Sergeant Carter! Visitors for the Lieutenant!'

'Now they'll even know in Ogdensburg,' said Duncan as he ducked under an archway. 'No wonder nothing ever stays a secret.'

When the lieutenant saw the letter he made quick arrangements to have them taken to the colonel's house. But they didn't see the colonel immediately. As they approached the house they were taken around the side, entering through a summer kitchen, where an orderly took the letter. 'Wait here for me. The colonel has guests to supper.' He disappeared into the main part of the house, and their shepherd, duty done, retraced his steps towards the fort.

The hum of conversation filtered out to where they stood, accompanied by the sound of cutlery on china. Perhaps the latter acted as catalyst, for Duncan's stomach gave a loud gurgle, and Cameron also suddenly became aware of his own hunger. 'Will they give us the slops, d'you think?' asked Duncan. 'Man, I could even eat that horse that brought me here.'

But the orderly reappeared even before Cameron could answer him and led them through to a small slip room behind the stairs. 'You'll wait here until the Colonel calls for you.'

'Is it likely to be long? We haven't eaten yet.' Duncan was persistent in his attention to his needs.

But the orderly was used to what must be a constant stream of people coming and going on business. 'I cannot tell you. And nor have I.' He disappeared.

As the youths sat on a bench, Duncan looked around at the room and its sparse furnishings, and gave a large sigh. 'No space at the table for us. And I was so looking forward to dining with the Colonel.'

Cameron laughed. 'It would be your first time ever with someone so important - you'd probably drop everything at least once.'

'Aye, man. But at least I'd not be so damned hungry. The Colonel would understand.'

But at that moment the orderly reappeared with a couple of plates in hand. 'Bread and salt pork. Be thankful.'

Duncan nodded, but looked disgustedly at Cameron as the latter gave him a hefty kick. Cameron knew he'd been about to ask for ale.

It took the Colonel another couple of hours to see his guests away. Cameron had heard toasts being drunk, not only to the King, but also to the President, which meant that an American officer was present. He found it strange that a British officer-in-command was prepared to entertain American officers at dinner, and that the same officers would pass on a message that effectively turned the cannon away from potential American targets, no matter whose they were. But it was not an officer class he aspired to, so he did not pay them much attention.

After dinner the guests had stayed talking and smoking, and both Duncan and Cameron dozed, tired from the travel and warmed from the food within them. It was the Colonel himself who woke them. 'I would shoot a sentry who slept on duty.'

'Our apologies, sir. It has been a long day.' Cameron managed to put the words in before Duncan said something inane. His first waking moments were never lucid.

'So you are Cartwright's boys. Well, come through to my parlour.' He glanced at their boots before he said it, but must have been satisfied with their state.

They found that he'd read the letter, because it was lying opened on the table beside his reading chair, a lamp casting an orange stain across Mr Richard's looping hand. As he sat he pointed to the long truckle bed that lay against one wall. 'See if you can sit on that and stay awake for a while.' And as he said it Cameron realized that the term *parlour* had been used with slight amusement - it looked more like an officer's working quarters.

Cameron was slightly nervous, and said slightly more hastily than he'd intended: 'Colonel Cartwright says to tell you that he prefers potash, sir, even though it would do little to win the war.'

Macdonell looked puzzled for a moment, but then: 'Ah, iron or potash. Yes. I did ask him that.' He picked up the letter. 'I think my friend Richard is a little less than honest about potash's value to a wartime economy.' He looked at them. 'Which one is MacNeil?'

'I am, sir.'

'And you are articled to Colonel Cartwright.'

'Unofficially, sir. I'm learning the trade.'

'Hm. Well we need more of his kind in this young dominion, so learn it well. And you?' He shot this at Duncan.

'Articled to my friend, sir.'

The Colonel laughed at this. 'You probably cause most of the mischief that he pulls you out of, no?'

Duncan had the effrontery to be indignant. 'Sir!'

'No matter, young man. No matter. This whole war is nothing but a barrel of mischief. Though there is precious little to laugh about.' He waved the letter and looked at Cameron. 'Now, *you* tell me why you think we should think about iron for a moment.'

'We believe that there is a foundry being built at Glasgie.'

He stayed silent a moment. 'Perhaps I already know that.'

'Sir, this was intelligence we gave Colonel Cartwright and he sent us to see you.' There was little Cameron could do. He felt caught between two masters, on the one hand Mr Richard called for general intelligence, while Colonel Macdonell clearly wanted something more specific. This, he thought, meant that he had two separate jobs rather than one that was all-encompassing.

'Yes, he did. You are quite right. In fact, I asked him to.' He sat back, stroking his lips and chin with a forefinger, thumb under the chin and elbow beside him on the arm of the chair. 'Do you know any more than this?'

'Not much, sir. We believe iron ore has been found in considerable quantity, though we have not seen the workings.'

'As it would have to be to justify a foundry.'

'Yes, sir.'

'Mm.' He paused. 'I know of your father, young MacNeil, though do not know him well. A steady man, I think. One for these times. Yours,' and he looked at Duncan, 'has not come within my purview. What is he?'

'I am afraid, sir, that he has already passed away. Last winter's fever.'

'Ah. I'm sorry to hear it. So you are your mother's breadwinner now.'

Cameron thought Duncan had never heard it put in those terms. The response was quite sober. 'Yes, sir.'

'Well. I am going to tell you young men a story. And then we shall see whether you can help me with it.' He leaned back in his chair as a child's grandfather might at the telling of a winter tale. 'There is a level at which war appears to be a game played on both sides. You see, any war requires money. Much of it tends to be levied against families such as your own, MacNeil, though you pay for it with service, perhaps. In other cases, it is given against future favours expected. But there are those who provide it as a commercial venture, who wish to profit from it financially, and who, in the best sense of insurance, hedge their bets. So they finance both sides.'

As the Colonel spoke Cameron remembered Mr Richard: *But God determines your profit, and against Him you play the underwriters.* If he was hearing correctly, the Colonel was about to tell them the name of an underwriter; certainly not of God, anyway, for there was so much havoc and chance in war, in this idiotic war, that only God could know its outcome.

'So we have a gentleman, of good family and fortune, who has a variety of interests in various parts of the world. He has made investments in this neck of the woods, with a view to the long term - land purchases, trading house, schooners. But these are risky investments, and people are fickle, so he cannot see immediately what will be the return to him. It is pure speculation.' There was a glass of something on the small table beside the lamp, and he took a sip of it.

'But let us say that a government needs money to finance a venture of its own. Now, the government, in its *personae*, may seem unsteady and poorly led. But its cause is generally popular, and a government, in its *institutions*, may be held to account. So, while to the government the venture is pure speculation, to the financier it is rock solid - he knows that he will see his money.'

'Our friend wishes all parties to understand that he holds no particular allegiance to the government, because he is not a citizen of that nation. Yet he is resident in that very same country, enjoying all the opportunities open to him to make money. His wealth, as long as he keeps it, protects him from most contingencies. He may call upon almost all as his protectors. Do you follow me so far?'

Cameron thought he knew where this was heading. He wasn't sure about Duncan, because he could not discuss Mr Richard's business with anyone, but knowing Duncan he had little reason to believe that his friend saw some of the more distant ramifications of the war. But they both nodded.

'Glasgie is this man's investment. He also owns most of St Lawrence County, either outright or through mortgage. And as you both know we can put a cannonball across the river and directly into some of his properties.' He paused. 'He has asked us to protect that property.'

'I thought he was no longer trading with Montreal, sir.'

The Colonel smiled. 'So you know of whom I speak, MacNeil. Good. Let us say that the embargo has him constrained in that direction but that private enterprise is rife. He can bring in goods from any direction he wishes, or buy from anyone who does. However, I think it's true to say that he feels he has no protection on the river, not from us anyway, and so does not tempt fate too often. And remember, he lost a large amount of money when those scows were wrecked in the rapids. He does not like the river.'

He stopped, and Cameron thought that he was going to tell them to go, that he'd see them in the morning - he looked tired, but whether it was age or the stress of the war Cameron could not tell. But the Colonel was hunting in a pocket for something. He came out with a small box, opened it, pinched some snuff from it, and then took half a minute to settle down from its effects. As he stored a handkerchief, he said: 'Your man apparently began the works at Glasgie in support of his settlement plans - settlers require tools, wagon wheels, pots. But his settlers are incapable of paying their rents let alone buying hoes and ploughshares, so he will still have to give them all on credit. He

61

needs that foundry to provide him some other source of income. What better than to supply the inputs of war to a nation that will borrow from him to buy them?'

Cameron had smiled inwardly at the *your man*. 'Cannonballs, sir,' he said, without a smile. Cameron was beginning to dislike this snakelike tale.

The Colonel nodded. 'So you will understand where I am headed. What *is* there at Glasgie? Is the foundry working? Are they casting household items or implements of war? I think I want *you* to find out. He may be a gentleman, but I'll be damned if I'll protect a foundry making shot to fire at us.'

The trouble with avoided targets was that it smelled of connivance. Cameron didn't feel sorry for Mr Foster, but he thought that in this cross-border war, even with the very low probability of a direct hit, you should accept what the fates dealt you rather than try and prevent an outcome. Mr Foster's difficulty was that he had come into the north country with more money than anyone else, and so considered himself untouchable. Of European extraction, his only vested interest was interest; the sort that lending money gets you. He had bought up a great deal of this same north country with the expressed intention of making 5% on every transaction, whether it be for land, ploughshares or candles, and the war was making it harder to collect debts. But he'd obviously had a message for no-one invests in something so forlorn as the north country without the message that there is 5% to be made (the King was not considered; that's what the war was about); perhaps he received it directly from Armstrong, whom he certainly knew, though the former was probably not Secretary for War at the time the acquaintance was made. Nevertheless, it was a useful acquaintance, because Foster received the order for cannonball from Armstrong.

That was not all he received, though. Foster had a nephew, of whom there is one-way correspondence only, nephew-to-uncle, who trailed around behind his uncle, begging for the introduction that would bring fortune, and thus happiness, for only the former could bring the latter. There is not a chance in heaven that the nephew met Armstrong without his uncle's introduction, and relations appeared cordial enough for the young man to be invited to stay. There is nothing written about Mrs Armstrong, or any Masters Armstrong, but there were two other gifts apparently coming: a horse and a commission. In the 1st Dragoons, based in Syracuse.

Trouble

Gouverneur was also a frontier community in those days. So they came to Glasgie because of the ruts, which said that heavy wagons were still using the same road. They then headed west - the only place they could think of, in that direction, was Sackets Harbor, where the other wagons were heading and Chauncey was active.

Glasgie was alive with movement. He saw a load of saw-logs being heaved off a wagon, at doors which led into what appeared to be a smelting shed. Red-hot iron came out the other end, already formed roughly into the final product, sand-moulded, he presumed, inside, before being cast, transported, cool, into the finishing barns. There was evidence around of what this place would become, in the rope-demarcated stone foundations. He took shelter once again among trees on the bluff. The fact that no new snow had fallen worried him, for he thought he had the answer now that MacDonnell needed. He backed away trying to make it seem that his tracks were random, that he hadn't just come from Ogdensburg, because he knew that any patrol would find him, especially the Dragoons that, he thought, were just behind him. Any sort of track would lead them right to where he was hidden. But it was too late in the year for snow, and the wagons from the south were running on dirt.

He heard the jingling of horse harness before he expected to, but by that time they were on him and there was little he could do. He was about a mile east of the ironworks. Then he saw that he had trouble.

'Who are you?' The question was spoken with a disdain for the answer.

Cameron thought little about hiding his identity on this open border, but recognized the consequences of a lie and what he had been doing. He remained silent, blood still running down his arm. He kept it hidden.

'Loyalist or patriot?'.

And there was the problem, for the face he'd seen before aboard the *Periwinkle*. He kept silent.

The mounted officer, obviously a Dragoon, swung down from his horse. 'Answer me, dog'. He went to slap Cameron's face with his glove. He was about Cameron's age, but had the look of someone unused to toil.

A bit weedy, thought Cameron. He jumped back. 'None of your business', he replied.

'Oh, its like that, is it', said the other. The rest of the troop had been a bit slow to react - the combination of cold and what Cameron read as a dislike for the man - but soon swung down and pressed against Cameron.

'So, I'll ask you again,' said the American officer,' Loyalist or patriot.'

'Both' said Cameron, who couldn't see any difference, even though he knew the answer wanted.

'Ah, but you can't be both", said the American. 'You are one or the other. It's the way things are. We deal harshly with Loyalists. We've been following you quite a while.' Cameron saw the rope with the noose already tied behind his saddle. It left little to his imagination. He saw that the only means of escape were to dissemble. He was surprised that the other had seen him near Ogdensburg, but that gave him an idea.

'Just checking the bush for next spring. Attached to the Ogdensburg militia, sir'.

The Dragoon officer, who had been the only one to see him, and just chased him across-country, was not mollified and didn't give up immediately. 'Then where's your uniform?' He saw an easy opening, but it left Cameron with little escape.

'At home, sir. Didn't think I should wear it for such a mundane task. Not a military one.' Truer than you know, thought Cameron.

The Dragoon Captain was not really fooled; he'd got a good look at him before. Unlike his men, who were more interested in warmth.

'Ogdensburg, eh. I shall be dining with the Commander of the garrison tonight. I shall look for you there.' The Captain thought it would be simpler to unmask him there; have him shot as a spy. The question was just 'which side of the river was he from?'

Cameron didn't know any of this, and just thought the Dragoon was putting his stomach before duty; he thought this was quite frequent, and the muttering from the men seemed to confirm it. They paid him scant respect.

But Cameron did recognize that the sooner he put some miles between himself and this patrol the better; he hoped that Old Leggett had not been compromised. If this Dragoon went across the river, it would be even worse. There were still cross-river dinners. Which garrison might be host didn't bear thinking about. Nor did any other consequences.

'Who should I ask for, sir?'

'Daniel Harris, 1st Dragoons.' An idea was forming as Harris said it.

Cameron, for his part, thought he was home free.

Neil Thomas

Prejudice

The phone brought me back out of Cameron's world, but I carefully closed his second diary and put it on the bed before answering.

'Mr MacNeil.'

The voice I knew, but it was a second before I could put a name to it, and it was softer, silkier. 'Yes, Nancy. How are you?'

'Very well. I just happened to be passing, and thought I'd call you, to see whether you'd given my proposal any further thought.'

I hadn't. In fact I'd forgotten it completely, and I cursed myself for not having called the Dean and telling him I wanted nothing to do with it. 'No, I haven't,' I said, again without thinking, 'but was...'

'Perfect. Perhaps we could talk about it a little more. I'm here downstairs. Could we meet for a drink?'

I knew I'd have to put some effort into turning it all around before I could walk away from it, so I said 'Give me five minutes, then. In the lobby?'

'In the bar.'

It was not a bar I'd had a drink in, and one look around it confirmed that it was unlikely I'd change the habit. But there were only couples at the low tables, doing their mingling quietly. Elevator music flowed out of the ceiling.

I turned, thinking that she must be in the lobby after all, but she was beside me suddenly, coming out of the shadowed passage from the washrooms. I still could not remember her surname, so had no means of maintaining a formal distance, and my

`Hello, Nancy,' sounded as lame to me as it must have sounded collegial to her.

She read it as quartering the distance between us, and took my arm. `I'd much rather eat out, wouldn't you?'

I wouldn't have intended any such thing, but I hadn't eaten, and a decision on the evening meal had been imminent. Suddenly deciding that, for once, a Princess Street dinner would be better shared, even with Nancy, I nodded. It would just take me a little longer to withdraw from her proposal.

Perhaps my prejudices should occasionally lay themselves to rest. She did not raise her idea once in the subsequent two hours. Dinner, in a restaurant a little way off Princess Street that Nancy suggested we try, which was definitely more secluded than my regular high-street hangouts, was good, and there seemed to be none of the insecure figure I thought I'd detected before. She was attentive and I found myself enjoying her company. Talk drifted between many things.

At one point she said: 'It's hard being a woman in my field. You're not taken seriously. Chauvinism dies hard among engineers.'

'Women are not expected to get their hands dirty?'

'Not just that. They're not expected to understand engineering - any branch of it. It's a male dominion. At Queen's, and especially in the undergraduate fraternity, engineers drink harder and faster than anyone else. If you can't keep up, it's taken to prove the point.'

'No such thing as a temperate engineer?'

'Only when they have to go on the wagon later on.'

'Are you a Queen's graduate?'

'No. I studied in Montreal. McGill.'

'Did you like the city?'

'I miss it now - makes me understand how much I undervalued it then.'

'Kingston's a bit dull.'

'A single woman is very likely to remain single.'

'Candidates lacking in volume or quality?'

'Generally lacking in style. Not enough Latin blood, perhaps. All grey, a bit like the limestone.'

I understood, then, that her shell was just that, a greyness adopted in order to fit in, leaving only her obvious gender for her professional colleagues to deal with.

It was quite dark by the time we finished, but the evening was warm. We meandered south under the streetlights, and then seemed automatically to turn east. Within minutes the exposed foundations of old Fort Frontenac, the French bastion destroyed well before even the original Loyalists arrived, were shadows on our left, and we followed the curve of the tall limestone wall on our right, round to the causeway. A couple of cadets from the Royal Military College walked past us at a quick march.

'Late for curfew, d'you think?' asked Nancy.

'Probably forbidden to walk any other way,' I said. Nancy laughed.

The Cataraqui river was calm under us as we crossed it, the water six feet below us, bringing out of the night everything that fell on this side of the height of land; on the other it went to Ottawa. We stopped to look down into it, but I saw nothing, not even ghosts.

Beyond the causeway the triumphal arch at the old gates slipped past us in the night, and we were soon on the road climbing the slope to the east of Navy Bay. The College lay silent on its western edge, lights on in a few windows. Fort Henry loomed slowly from the ground beside us, a simple gray wall with embrasures at regular intervals. As we reached the top, and stopped, the Fort came to attention, sullen in the night. No sound from within came over the walls.

We walked beyond the peak to the grassy slope that looked over the river. Little of the city was visible to the west, just a glow in the sky over the Fort and beyond the College, and patches of light on the water where reflections carried the headlamp of the occasional car turning near the waterfront. We stood quietly for some moments, Nancy absorbed by the stars. I avoided looking at the Fort, traitor as it was to the history that most interested me.

Stew

After the Dragoons, it took a cautious hour to circle through the trees to a point where he finally had safe vantage. Care was necessary, for if this were indeed war materiel on the road, it would not be unguarded. There would be other scouts out in the bush on both sides of the column - or, if there weren't, then other knowledge was at work here, knowledge that knew there to be no threat. This was something in which Cameron felt he would not trust. His arm still hurt like hell.

At a safe half-mile he was surprised by what he saw. The southern road came from his left and curved straight away from him. Out of the south came a continual column of wagons, horses being whipped hard, harder certainly than they should have been, for there was ice in some places and they were having to haul their loads through the gullies in which water had still run under that ice. Cameron could see the carcasses of at least two animals that looked as though they'd dropped in harness, too close to the main trail to have been unhitched before they'd died, and as he watched he saw a drover, who was trying to drag his team across the rocks of a streambed, fall, and stay fallen. The horses, whipped by another man, who was being cursed by other drovers behind, ran right over him. They all had the look of being pressed, men and horses both, with no latitude for easy travel. It looked increasingly certain that General Armstrong had indeed written his letter.

It had ceased snowing some days before, and though it was spring the country was still in the grip of cold. They rode the horses down off the high ground, ploughing step by step through belly-high drifts. The height over Glasgie had offered no vantage, and the level of noise not before heard in that part of the country since they'd begun their peregrinations compelled them to investigate. Shouts, stamping of hooves, jingling harness, multiplied by a factor they could not yet imagine - but loud enough to make them wonder what was on the road, and, they thought again, bound for Sackets Harbor.

'I do not think we should get close to this road.' Duncan, back with Cameron again, voiced his worry aloud, but Cameron's, after the Dragoons, was no less worried. 'Let us move parallel to it until we can see through the bush.'

One thing was certain - that there were heavy wagons on that road. Cameron cautioned Duncan to wait a moment, giving that sound all his attention. And as he listened he could slot the shouts of different drovers into segments of an arc, and that arc was definitely rotating to the northwest. 'Bound for Sackets Harbour.' Cameron said.

'So has it begun?' asked Duncan, though looking for no answer from his companion. For he meant the inevitable consequence of a large movement in time of war.

But Duncan knew they should want better confirmation than noises in the bush to inform their masters that the American Secretary of War saw threat or opportunity on his northwestern frontier.

'Do you wait here,' Cameron said, 'with the horses.' The pain in his arm was not going to stop him now.

But while these two young men were ostensibly officers of His Majesty's Army, Mr Richard was still the key to what they could do. Old Leggett, Samuel and Jeremiah, among others, were his men. That is to say, they sold to him and borrowed from him. Occasionally he made it easy on them, in fact paid them a *commission*, when they brought him what he wanted. Before the war this had been simple commercial intelligence: What land was being cleared? Had the ashes been gathered? Then: How had the wheat grown? Was there a surplus? And he'd made his preparations for shipments to Montreal. Now, with the war, it was little different - the client was right to hand. The Army (and Navy) had many mouths.

But the young men saw Old Leggett, Samuel and Jeremiah as theirs. Simply put, they became the steps required at certain points along a path sketched as the youths' lifeline. At one point Cameron likened it to the one on his hand - it were little different, certainly as irregular. But if he had never had the courage to have *that* one read, especially after Alice, *this* one he read with great care, cognizant of weaknesses easily introduced by lack of foresight. Again, simply put, they needed three burrows for safe travel; Old Leggett, Samuel and Jeremiah afforded them. Should anything go wrong, they should be confident (oh, how he wished he'd read *that* lifeline) that the land afforded them the means to reach their burrows in safety.

So their path ran across the American mainland just downriver from Gananoque, southwest to Sackets Harbor. And while Colonel McDonnell had the area to the east well covered from Prescott, Old Leggett also kept his ear to the ground for any news.

They were back at Jeremiah's place by dark. Their horses were his, stout shaggy beasts that could pull a plough for hours. It was safer to be seen on a ploughhorse than a charger, though neither youth had ever ridden a charger. In the snow, a ploughhorse was also safer to ride, plate-sized hooves to grip any ice below.

'Well?' Jeremiah would not wait for them to give the news in their own time. He hated his government's policies with such a passion that he required his foreknowledge to be fed before he'd feed them, though he wasn't to feed them tonight. His small barn, well hidden some distance from his cabin, was warm, heated by the five cows he kept there, and two other horses besides the ones they'd ridden. Early kittens tumbled in the hay manger, right under the cows' noses.

'Heavy traffic from Utica. Probably fifty to an hundred wagons a day northwest to the Harbor.' said Duncan.

'I knew it!' Jeremiah would have been puce with anger had the light been strong enough to show it. As it was he was one step from foaming at the mouth. 'And where do you think the monies will come from to pay for it? Not from the south, where they declared this little game. Oh no! Right here. We shall soon have news of the levy. You wait and see.'

But they couldn't, so they moved their saddles to the other two horses in the barn, Samuel's, and said their goodnights.

Samuel gave them their dinner late that night, a mess of salt pork and peas that probably put a tidy end to the remnants of his winter stores. The pork had a bluish tinge. A glance from Duncan to Cameron at one point was easily read: how has he survived on *this*? But Samuel was more complacent than Jeremiah, and expected, for favours given, for them to be the same. They collected old Leggett's horses and rode on; Cameron's arm began to hurt less.

'There is word that they *will* manufacture cannonball at Glasgie'. Old Leggett spared not a smile.

Cameron looked at him with a light grin. 'I saw some today.' The bound arm was evident.

'The ironworks are that advanced?' asked Leggett.'They have moulds?'

'They appear not to be waiting for the stone works,' said Cameron. 'They have thrown up some wooden shelters.' He did not say that the obvious hurry meant that no-one yet had thought of horseshoes yet coming from Glasgie. 'Foster must have had the nod from Washington.'

`They say Foster is trying to undercut Oswego.'

Cameron thought a moment. `They will not have wasted any more horses than they already have bringing cannonball from the south. Perhaps Oswego cannot meet the demand the government is foreseeing. You are sure this is competition and not lack of supply?'

`I cannot say.' Old Leggett never went beyond his knowledge, even if there were hearsay. Interpretation was left to others.

`Has MacDonnell heard of this yet?'

`I cannot say that, either.'

Though it was a coincidence that Jeremiah, Samuel and Old Leggett were single men. Something about solitude had made them Cartwright's, that and their disgust with their southern kinsmen, though they were kinsmen in nationality alone. But both Samuel and Old Leggett had both been married, the former a bystander of infidelity and flight, the latter of death. Perhaps, in that way that any marriage will temper a man, they saw further than Jeremiah, knew the range of suffering war will bring; Jeremiah's passions were always on the surface, simple hates, direct solutions. Samuel and old Leggett knew that there were few solutions easily found, and that they could do only little to find them. To them there was no concept of `side'; they were onlookers even locally, too old to be in any militia, and in the broader sense the war was a tide sweeping over them.

Memories

Little Penny lay on her stomach staring into the depths of the river, where fronds of weed growing on the river bed stood immobile in the scarcely moving current, and, she hoped, a fish might pass under her nose. David sat under a tree, ferns and seedling maples around him, watching Penny. I tidied up the mooring lines, enjoying the early autumn sun on my neck.

Call it a whim, one of those moments that hit you, when you decide your mind is saturated and there is an urgent, though not necessarily rational, need to do something entirely different. So I'd rented the dinghy, and phoned the house. Penny had answered, big woman in a little body, and had apparently sat listening to the subsequent conversation.

But it was not completely a whim, because there was something deep within me that wanted to visit the place where that first murder had occurred, a sense of smell, perhaps, which thought it might find a scent to an improbable solution.

The river was in one of its complacent moods, a light southwesterly breeze giving us a downwind run over stippled water, and leaving ample time for contemplation of the banks of Howe and Wolfe Islands, places not so far distant from the time when the first Loyalists took property and began the reconstruction of shattered lives. Most of the shore was low, giving long upward views inland, though rockfaces of Precambrian granite gave the eastern end of Howe the look of the flank of a dragon, guardian, perhaps, of the western door to the Thousand Islands.

The Thousand Islands is one of those places where creation left a clear message: some things should not be tame; life should not be simple. Though Man's effort to provide safe passage through the upper St Lawrence has done much to break that primordial spirit, and most of the islands sit in waters as gentle as a pond. But it was not like that then, when vessels were lost in the spring-torn rage of rapids, or on the tooth of a rock springing from the riverbed to claim its due from poor navigation in a thunderous storm.

Strangely, the island I wanted was like none of the rest, the sole limestone slab left lying on granite underpinning, flat from end to end; *a garden in the tangle of wild*, Cameron called it. Shovel Island, the one ignominious name on the official list, which read like a Burke's Naval Peerage. But someone must have had a sense of humour, for Sir Cloudesley Shovel drowned with his fleet off the Scilly Isles, victim of, or perhaps responsible for, execrable navigation. Shovel Island would never sink anybody. It didn't sink us.

'I'm hungry, Granpa. You promised we'd eat as soon as we got here.' Penny's attention had wandered from fish to birds, and she was watching a wheeling gull as she spoke.

'Bring the basket, pet, and spread the tablecloth over there on the grass.'

'Give me the basket, Aster. My arm's too short to reach.' There was hunger in the demand on that earnest little face. The basket was heavy enough to make her strut as she made her way over to the grass-covered headland. I followed behind, hungry also.

I hadn't told David why we'd come here. The phone call was for a day on the river, picnic somewhere, Penny invited. 'You're providing the boat? Why didn't you say earlier? We could have used mine. It's been ages since I put it in the water.' But even if I hadn't borrowed the boat, the sandwiches came from the same house.

'Drink, Granpa. I'm thirsty.'

The grass was soft, not like the *puna*, where it was spiky and grew in clumps, and one walked around it rather than through it. But this clear St Lawrence fall sky brought the cobalt blue of the High Andes crashing back into my mind. There, the path had been made even more tortuous by surface water that lay in some of the broader open plains between the hills. These were still the foothills to higher peaks, though we had been above forty-five-hundred metres. I'd had to stop several times, my blood still short of the extra red corpuscles needed to scrape every milligram of oxygen out of the rarified atmosphere, and my heart not the extra-large muscular organ of the Andean peasant.

'What's the matter, Alastair?'

I came out of it with a snap, heart pounding, breathing hard. The trigger had been unexpected, not the continuous remembrance of events that haunted me daily, but something that slammed me right back into it, so that I had been there rather than here. God knows what must have been on my face.

'Sorry, David. I got distracted. Unpleasant memory.'

'Peru?'

'I had some trouble, and I'm afraid it comes back now and again. It did so just then.'

'That limp?'

I nodded. 'Last traces of a beating.' At least they hadn't put a bullet through the kneecap.

'Do you want to talk about it?'

And there was the problem. Sunny day, picnic, gentle water at the foot of the rock. How could I destroy it with the memories of pig-hate and slaughter?

'I'm not sure that I can - it's very hard to talk about. Perhaps too deeply buried for the moment.' .... Though I didn't mention it at the time, there's another reason why we're here today. I'd rather talk about that.' And there were little ears present, too, though I didn't know whether that older death would be less terrifying than the recent, modern ones.

But David was still thinking of Peru, his mind perhaps back to an unfinished dinner conversation, and he presented me with a doorway. 'Tell me a little about the people. How different are they?'

'Different? Very. Mostly very gentle, with lives tied to subsistence.' I remembered another woman, sitting, legs stretched, straining against the rope. They'd hammered pegs into the ground at the end farthest from her, and tied off the warp ends like the foot end of a hammock. The head end was stretched evenly across her lap, the warp lines like the strings of a harp, and she shot the shuttle from side to side, swaying backwards and forwards as she lifted and dropped alternate warp sets, using a stick to keep them separated. A rope around her back kept the tension throughout the weaving, which, in the village square, against the soil, looked like a punk bandaid against a very ancient scalp.

'Are they very poor?'

'Probably as poor as the dispossessed Loyalists who came here.' Other women had been doing the same, weaving coarse matting from local fibres stained with garish modern dies. Baskets and sacks of the same material, for carrying market produce once a week down the valleys into town, were scattered around. Potatoes, oca, olluco, quinoa, lima beans, all the produce of a peasant economy which subsisted on the barren hills of severely eroded Andean mountainsides, four thousand metres above sea level. Below the waist the women were as garish as their creations, the same dyes echoed in their flounced skirts which barely reached below their knees. More sedate woollen jumpers continued a trend which terminated in uniformly dull brown bowler hats perched above sets of long pigtails. Some of the pigtails bore coloured strands which denoted marital status. It wasn't a code I'd had much direct interest in learning.

`But the Loyalists were able to create wealth. After a generation or two, many of them were well off.'

I nodded. `The Andes is more hostile.' So I talked about the *puna*, home to the llama and alpaca, both camels, and economic lifeblood to the local people. If the alpaca gave high quality wool, it was the llama that carried it and a good part of the crop harvest to the market centres. But camels do not have hooves, and don't do the damage that cattle and sheep do to grassland, so our path, at an altitude where there were very few cloven hooves, had been where we walked, not what we followed. I shuddered again.

Perhaps David saw it, and looked for something else. `Is that why we're here?'

`What?'

`Beatings. Perhaps murder?

I looked surprised. Then I remembered something. `Historical context?' The phrase that had gone over my head some nights before.

He smiled. `I was never privy to the details or to any of the material, but I heard the general story. Your grandfather was intrigued by it. I knew there were some diaries.'

`And later - Grandmother talked about it?'

`No, not really. All she would say was "It's Alastair's, now".'

`Keeping it in the family.'

`Something like that.'

I nodded. `There were five murders. Here, one of the five. The first.'

`On this island?'

`Somewhere on this island.' *He had been killed on the island, for he'd been waiting there for me. I found where his blood had run into the earth, but I found his body some distance away, under a loop of entrails from the belly tied in a lovers' knot around the low limb of a tree. His mouth was stretched with a stick into the semblance of a grin.*

`Who was it?'

'Cameron's partner.' I'd thought of him as Cameron so much, now, that I needed no other label. 'Perhaps then you know about Cameron MacNeil, a Lieutenant in the King's Border Scouts?'

'No more than his name. Knowing the importance he held for your grandparents it would have been rude to pry.'

'Does your history take in the Border Scouts?'

He smiled. 'Makes me sound a little old, doesn't it? But yes - I know that the Scouts were pulled together from the sons of the Loyalists who'd stood down in 1784. About twenty-five years later, when the families were well settled. Still the same King, of course.' He leaned back, taking a bite out of his sandwich. 'Who was his partner?'

'Duncan MacLeish. Also a son; I assume he was as knowledgeable about the river and the lands on both sides as Cameron had been.'

'Why was he killed?'

'Apparently as the first death in a chain intended to trap Cameron on the American side. Who did it, Cameron doesn't say.'

'The diaries aren't all inclusive? Remember, I know nothing of their contents.'

'The diaries describe why he was imprisoned, and the evidence on which he was hanged. If there is a clue to who actually did it, and why Cameron insisted on his innocence to the very end, I haven't found it. That's why they showed him no mercy; in court he refused to tell his story.'

'But what did they say? In the court, I mean.'

'The court decided that Cameron had Duncan killed, and arranged for the murder to look like a border skirmish. They took treason as the motive.'

'Treason?'

'I'll have to go back a bit to explain that. Cameron's family came up in the original wave of Loyalists.' Grandfather's notes had been thorough. My early school years had taught me some of the history, but, with professional interests elsewhere, I'd forgotten most of it. ' They'd been tenants in the Mohawk Valley, in northwest New York, and had, in fact, only recently before made the journey out from Scotland. It seems that his father's regiment, the Loyal Highlanders, was disbanded in the general stand-down of 1784, and its members settled as a group in Cataraqui Township Number One - what later became Kingston.

David nodded. 'Those were difficult early years for all Loyalists, though as soon as the communities throughout Upper Canada were reasonably well established there were waves of new American immigrants.'

'So not all the Loyalists had left?'

'Oh, yes. These were people with no particular political allegiance, but who thought that economic prospects were better on the British side of the river, or who had ties of family or friendship with the original Loyalists. It wasn't long before the original Loyalist refugees were outnumbered four-to-one.'

'So the Loyalists were really a very small group.'

'Small, but influential. Most held on to positions of authority within their communities, and were key figures once hostilities restarted in 1812.'

'That's a war I understand less.'

'It had two curious characteristics. It was begun largely because America was angry with Britain over maritime controls over trade with Europe. Remember, Britain was at war with France. But it was really a war kindled by the southern states of the Union; there was a lot of concern over British alliance with the Indian nations and the effects this might have on American expansion west and north. Funnily enough, the northern states were not interested in declaring war, but they were outvoted.'

'It must have made community relationships difficult if there were more Americans than Loyalists.'

'Loyalties were more complex, though the majority seemed, by then, to feel membership with the original refugees. Most communities had their own militia, commanded by those officers from the regiments disbanded in 1784. But there were anomalies. The Canadian Volunteers for one.'

'Canadian Volunteers? A community militia?'

'No. Canadian Volunteers to the Americans. Perhaps because of the cross river trade, some Canadians supported the American position. It was a unit particularly active in the Niagara Peninsula, causing havoc wherever it could and generally helping the American cause. Some of those that went to the other side had even been members of the Upper Canada Assembly.'

It was not hard, even almost two hundred years later, to conjure visions of both small and large vessels on these waters. Redcoats and cannon. It was a day to see history.
'There must have been rivalries within rivalries. Not only was there the race between

Kingston and the American Sackets Harbour, but also the King's Border Scouts and the Sackets Rangers. Cameron was accused of being a double agent, using his position in the King's Border Scouts to provide information to the Rangers.'

'But why the murders? Especially the first?'

'The court thought that Duncan had uncovered Cameron's plan, and that Cameron killed him to prevent him telling.' If there was anything in the diaries which spoke of the improbability of this, other than the cry from the heart implicit in the unadorned facts, and the worry for the wife and son of a soon-to-be-hanged man, it was the various matters of honour. *Duncan brought me out of more than one event on a life-thread; how, in God's name, could I have taken his?* 'It seems that politics got in the way of justice; the Navy made a mess of its race with Sackets Harbour and a scapegoat was needed. Cameron became it.'

But Duncan's was only the first death; and to tie the case together there had to be four more. And between each there was that symbol that made the connection easy to make. But the irony was that Cameron *had* killed Duncan: *Oh, the agony of an accident, and the knowledge that I was ten minutes late. Had I been on time at least he I might have saved.* In the end he decided that he had a price to pay before the one of duty, or perhaps that duty was included, to his wife and son.

I, on the other hand, killed three that I knew of, and had been denied the same method of payment. I think David saw me go, in the silence that followed, and he left me there, because the trail became clear, and I remembered Carlos' admonishment, that I was mad.

Penny was the one who broke it, though when she jumped on my back I thought it was a mountain-top Incan god bringing retribution, and I scared the wits out of her with my shout. That woke up David, who'd dozed off to somewhere more peaceful. But if he saw the reason in my eyes, he said nothing about it. 'Pet, you made Alastair jump.'

'Sorry, Aster,' and those little arms around my neck and the kiss on the cheek brought out my sorrow in a flood of tears quite different from the ones I'd shed for Grandmother. Penny, heartbrokenly thinking she was the cause, ran for a paper napkin, and spent the next minute wiping them off my face, as I wiped hers.

'Cameron's outfit used scouting tactics where they worked in pairs. He and Duncan had been together since the war started, and each was wounded in encounters with Indian scouts working for the Americans, but they survived because of friendship, bringing each other through it.' It was, ironically, an Indian method, picked up by the *Canadiens* long before the British used it, but the local sons of the soil knew of it and why it worked, and had insisted that if they were to be the Scouts then the Scouts would work that way. They knew of the past follies of rigid redcoat tactics.

We were halfway back to Kingston now, two hours of upwind tacks into a fresh breeze, and Oak Point visible on the north shore of Wolfe. Beyond was the hump of Fort Henry, the red-roofed grey limestone battlements a raspberry beret on the crest of the hill. Penny was asleep on a blanket in the bow, sun slanting across her face, arm across her eyes. Between us, David and I had settled into a rhythm, tacks made smoothly on a quiet ` helm's alee.' Peru stayed away, and I went on summarizing Grandfather's analysis.

` But there was considerable doubt about secrecy of movement, so the Scouts generally established a cross-border departure point only known to themselves. Cameron and Duncan had chosen Shovel Island for that night, planning to move island to island across the St Lawrence, testing the air before they made the mainland. Cameron had an accident and had to shoot his horse before he got to the farm where he was going to leave it. He was ten minutes late. But Duncan must have been half an hour early.'

` He knew it was as little as that? Duncan had not been dead longer?'

` They were both used to death, even if it was only a slaughtered animal.' *But his lips were still soft when I removed the stick, and I could ease the face into gentler repose.*

` But he found no sign of who'd done it.'

` None. But at that point he thought it was an Indian death.'

` The entrails?'

` Duncan was alive when his belly was cut open. And when he was scalped.'

David winced. ` Someone who wanted him to think it an Indian death?'

` That came later. Cameron made a search of the island, but he was alone and had to be careful. It took him an hour.' *I was never more a wraith than I was that night.* ` If they knew he was coming, as they must have, leaving him alone eventually signed his death warrant. The court could accept no reason for his not being attacked.'

` He was arrested immediately?'

` No. He took the body back to the shore, with instructions to a local family to pass a message to Kingston. Then he went back to the island and followed the original plan, alone.' *And I found the trail that had so carefully been prepared for me, the path perhaps unto death.*

So often at this time of year late afternoon squalls broke across the river, and I caught the line coming up off the lake, whipping the treetops along the western end of Wolfe and breaking across into the smaller river. I warned David and snapped the mainsheet from the jamming cleat. He grabbed Penny and put her on the centre thwart between us. 'Sorry, pet. It's going to get windy.' Penny rubbed a sleepy eye and nestled back into her grandpa's side, secure in the high collar of her lifejacket, no concern on her face at all. The sail became a sail, a hard fight across the river, and a final tack into the sheltered water behind the breakwater of Portsmouth Harbour.

By the time the dinghy was put away and the sails stored, Penny was awake and hungry again, and only the promise of a hot dog would satisfy that little mind. So David left the car at my hotel and we walked up the street I was coming to know so well. The squall had passed, late afternoon sun drying old limestone walls, and we ended up in the courtyard of some early nineteenth-century merchant, testing different combinations of mustard, relish and whatever else was on the table beside the barbecue, until Penny was sure we'd agreed that her choice was the best.

The sun was warm on my face, and the shelter from the wind and the beer that had gone down with the hotdog were both warming and relaxing body and mind. David, too, looked as though he'd had a needed break, the tiredness that had been evident since I'd known him dissolved a little. His world was Penny, evident in the care and comfort he provided both mother and daughter, and I began wondering about Penny's other parent, the one never mentioned. David glanced up, but if he thought he saw my thoughts he said nothing. Instead, he put some money on the table, 'My treat,' and gathered Penny and her things together. 'I think we'll go home.'

Angela was in the front garden when we reached the house, raking up the fall's first harvest of maple leaves, a serene woman at one with the day. She walked over to the car as we got out. Penny was fast asleep in the back seat, so she stretched in and lifted her out, not wanting to wake her. With just a smile she took her indoors.

David surprised me. 'Come to the back garden with me.'

We walked along the west wall, the sun, earlier, still strong enough for the wall to have soaked up some warmth. It now gave back that warmth to us.

'This was Mary's.' And 'this' was a scrambling orgy of rose bushes, an extension of the order of the front garden, but a touch of mayhem keeping it from being too perfect. Most were in a late fall foliage, some with leaves turning russet brown, some a more sinister red, a few hips here and there, and a few last blooms. But they were not the roses of most garden catalogues; these were as primitive as the land on which they grew

`Do you know your explorer's, Alastair?'

I stood looking at one rambler that looked as if a hand had never touched it, and wondered where he was going with such an esoteric train of thought. `You mean the early Europeans? Frobisher? Hudson?'

`Yes. Baffin.' He pointed at the one I was looking at. `And Cabot, Davis. All these.' And he gestured at the bushes that were carefully tended, even as they were wild. `Better roses than any of the hybrid teas or floribundas. Their flowers come to you from the heart of nature itself. Oh, bred, to be sure, but closer to a gift than any of the modern roses of the south. Named after those explorers.'

It was an interesting contrast, in this man that I'd seen as a closeted academic, an historian. Perhaps that was the link, Explorers with a large E, a channel to the past that he loved and lived, but closer, in fact, to the one I was living. And we went around, David putting names to the ones remaining. `Better when they are in bloom, of course, because then they show you their magic. But that is six months away, now. This,' and he pointed to a smaller, entirely more primitive bush, `will be the first we'll see. *Rosa hugonis*, named after a Jesuit priest, and brought out of China. Small, single yellow flowers in mid-May. Only then do I accept that spring has come, even though we've already had the daffodils. Then come all the others, and I rediscover Canada.'

But I thought the truth was that then he relived the time when his wife had been alive and they kept this wildness together. With the river behind, it would have seemed a charmed time. I understood that to have been shown the garden was a privilege.

Wolfe Island stretched flat along the horizon, funnel to whatever weather or ships came off the lake and into the Canadian side of the St Lawrence. Now, clear of the squall that had crashed through earlier, the river was home to a swarm of red-sailed dinghies, fighting among themselves for the evening breeze and heading for the inflated markers that showed the course. There was no clear view of Fort Henry to the east, other houses in the way, but I didn't need to see it to know it was there, looking down over Navy Bay, fooling one into accepting its self-imposed historic importance. But the *St Lawrence*, all one hundred plus guns of her, had rotted and was already serving her role as a pier footing when Fort Henry's majesty finally crowned that height of land, the really important history already over. Colonel By, the energy behind military fortification in Upper Canada at the time, was never forgiven the excessive cost.

`Do you know much about Yeo and Chauncey, David?'

He smiled. `More about Eckford, Gildersleeve and Dennis, really. As Commodores, Yeo and Chauncey each spent most of the war too worried about how much bigger his foe would build his next ship to achieve any major military gain. Even Chauncey's sacking of York was not the victory the Americans like to believe, because it had no strategic value. He was too afraid of Kingston's strength to attack where he would really have done some damage. Eckford and Gildersleeve were the ones that gave Chauncey his ships; Dennis was Yeo's man. They were all men who could build leviathans in wood in less than six months. Their's was the history.'

Their's was the history, ordinary men with great skills. But the death was Cameron's, because Yeo did not live up to the promise his appointment had brought. *He had made his fame in small ship battles and coastal landings, mettle sorely needed here, but perhaps when they made him Knight Commander of the Portuguese Order of St Benedict, his head took a different shape. Had we built an hundred small ships each with a single long gun we should have wrought more havoc than they will achieve with that monster taking shape in Navy Bay.* And Cameron never knew it, but Yeo had Dennis start on two more after that, not quite as large, but equally destined never to bring return to the investment. At least the *St Lawrence* took to her river; His Majesty's Ships *Canada* and *Wolfe* rotted in frames on their stocks.

`And Dennis?'

`I don't know what happened to him. Gildersleeve, at least, went back to his Atlantic business, taking his men with him. Eckford probably did the same.'

Angela had joined us, but was excluded by all we had discussed before, though she had been quiet, listening to us. David suggested: `Tell Angie about Cameron.' So, over more wine, in those chairs that wanted you in them, I recounted the story.

And when finally I finished, I walked back to my hotel, talking to both Cameron and my ghosts as the first hard frost began to bite the night.

Traitor

THE KINGSTON COURT MARTIAL

5-6 June 1814

Lieutenant Cameron MacNeil, King's Border Scouts

At a Court Martial convened on board His Majesty's Ship Royal George in Navy Bay on the fifth Day of June and continued by Adjournment until the following day

Present

Sir James Lucas Yeo, K.C.B. Commodore and Commander in Chief of His Majesty's Ships and vessels employed on the Lakes of Canada - - - President

Others

Excerpts of Minutes taken at the Court Martial

Lieutenant Cameron MacNeil was brought in and Audience admitted.

The Members of the Court before they proceeded to Trial respectively took the Oaths enjoined and directed by an Act of Parliament made and passed in the twenty second Year of the Reign of His late Majesty King George the second entitled 'An Act for amending, explaining, and reducing into one Act of Parliament the Laws relating to the Government of His Majesty's ships, Vessels and Forces by Sea.'

Then the attested Originals of two Letters dated the 1st June 1814, from Commodore Isaac Chauncey of the USS Superior and from Captain Stephen Popham late of His Majesty's Ship Magnet were read and are hereto annexed.

Lieutenant Cameron MacNeil, His Majesty's Border Scouts, sworn.

The Court asked.

Q. Was the Enemy enabled to take possession of the British Squadron after only a short action?

A. It was a short action, yes.

Q. Was it by your understanding that Captain Popham believed that the Enemy Force could be easily taken?

A. It was said I had given Captain Popham that intelligence two days before.

Q. State your reasons for believing this intelligence accurate?

A. It was not my intelligence. I have no reason to believe any accuracy.

Q. Do you agree that your intelligence was the sole reason for the loss of His Majesty's Force to the Enemy?

A. I was not witness to the full engagement therefore cannot attest to a sole reason for the loss. I state again that it was not my intelligence.

Q. Did you witness part of the action?

A. Yes.

Q. State it to the Court?

A. Under Commodore Chauncey's Order I was conveyed to Sandy Creek where I witnessed an action already enjoined. I noted at least one of Captain Popham's gunboats disabled by the time I arrived, and saw the remainder taken.

Q. Was the attacking force already in dire straits when you arrived?

A. I judged so, yes.

Q. Did the Action continue long thereafter?

A. It was over within the hour.

Q. And you saw Mr Hoare, master's-mate of the His Majesty's Ship Montreal, killed?

A. I saw him already fallen. I did not witness the event of his death.

Mr John Gallen, Bosun of the Gunboat Lois called in and sworn

The Court asked.

Q. How came you to escape the Action?

A. I was able to slip over the side at the moment in which our vessel was forced to yield.

Q. How did you manage to regain the British shore?

A. I am the Fleet swimming champion. I judged it important to return with news of the Action and was able to use the natural features of the American shore to hide.

Q. How long did it take you?

A. Three days and nights.

Q. State your view of the Action to the Court.

A. Once we entered the mouth of Sandy Creek, the masts of the enemy's boats were plainly visible over the marsh. Their not attempting to interrupt our entry into the creek confirmed Captain Popham's understanding that they were only protected by militia.

Q. State your reason for believing this?

A. His semaphore to Captain Spilsbury.

Q. Captain Popham continued the Action?

A. He took the boats within a quarter of a mile of the enemy and landed Lieutenant Cox of the royal marines and the principal part of his men on the left bank.

Q. Who was landed on the right?

A. Captain Spilsbury and Lieutenant Browne with the cohorn and small-arm party. Also Lieutenant McVeagh and a few marines.

Q. What did these parties?

A. They advanced on the flanks of the gunboats.

Q. Were the gunboats still firing?

A. They had dispersed a body of Indians, but as they made a turning of the creek opening the enemy's boats to our view the carronade was disabled.

Q. What did Captain Popham then?

A. He pulled the boat around to bring the 4-pounder to bear.

Q. Was this not effective?

A. I believe the enemy thought we were commencing our retreat. They advanced on us with about 150 riflemen, 200 Indians and a numerous body of militia and cavalry, which soon overpowered us.

Q. Did Captain Popham strike his colours then?

A. Captain Spilsbury was able for a time to check the advance by the fire which he kept up with the cohorn and his party.

Q. How great would you say were our losses?

A. I know Mr Hoare dead and Lieutenants Cox and McVeagh dangerously wounded. I believe some twenty dead overall and double the number wounded.

Lieutenant Cameron MacNeil recalled.

The Court asked.

Q. How do you account for the size of the enemy force?

A. I cannot express an opinion as I did not know the enemy's troop movements.

Q. Can you believe that the enemy did not know of Captain Popham's intended attack?

A. I cannot.

Q. Whom do you serve?

A. I serve the King.

Q. What service was it to His Majesty that you orchestrated the deaths of tens, and the capture of hundreds, of his men? Let alone significant materiel losses?'

A. I did not. My service was the identification of Woolsey's convoy.

Q. Was not Woolsey's convoy a trap?

A. Woolsey's convoy was essential to Commodore Chauncey's spring campaign, and was so designed. But it was admirable bait, and appears risked to spring a trap.

Q. Do you approve both of the Americans and of what they did? You say Commodore and admirable as if so.

A. My use of the term of rank is no more than the respect of a junior officer for one his senior, no matter from which side of the lake he fights.'

Q. But your admiration?

A. Only for a successful stratagem. Not for any gain it might have brought.

Decision

Pursuant to receipt of a Letter dated 1ˢᵗ of June 1814 from Commander Isaac Chauncey Commodore of the American Fleet at Sacketts Harbour and the Official Report of the same Date from Captain Stephen Popham late of His Majesty's Ship Magnet presently held at Commander Chauncey's Pleasure both detailing the particular circumstances of the defeat of Captain Popham's Expeditionary Force at Sandy Creek by an American Force under the Command of Mr Melancthon Woolsey The Court proceeded to enquire into the cause and circumstances of the Capture of Captain Popham and his

Force on the 30th May and to try Lieutenant Cameron MacNeil for his Conduct on the day prior to that Occasion and having heard the Evidence produced and compleated such Enquiry and having maturely and deliberately weighed and considered the whole The Court is of the opinion That the Capture of His Majesty's Force under Captain Popham's Command was principally the result of deliberate Treason on the part of Lieutenant Cameron MacNeil Captain Popham's Force having been deliberately misled into believing Mr Melancthon Woolsey travelled with scant defence So being able to overcome Captain Popham's Expeditionary Force with significant losses to Men & Materiel Which notwithstanding the conspicuous Zeal and Valour shewn by Captain Popham and his Men resulted in the lamentable fall of His Majesty's Expeditionary Force That Lieutenant Cameron MacNeil was solely to blame for the losses suffered That Lieutenant MacNeil deliberately transmitted to the Enemy the expected Movements of His Majesty's Force That Lieutenant MacNeil did not act with the Proper conduct expected of an Officer in His Majesty's Army of Upper Canada and the Court doth adjudge the said Lieutenant Cameron MacNeil guilty of the Charge brought and that he shall suffer the maximum Penalty for his Offence Which Hanging shall be carried out at Dawn on the 7th of this month.

Signed: *James Lucas Yeo, Bart.*

Pork

Before the war, the MacNeils had spent a lot of time just over the river in the north country. Mr MacNeil had many friends, and, travelling conditions being what they were, they often made more than a week of it. Mrs MacNeil sometimes went, too, though she was in eternal fear of baby Hilary's health so felt that she were better off staying at home. Mr MacNeil did not like this, for he was very much a family man, but Cameron was the only child of three so far to have reached his teens so he understood the wisdom of minimizing the extra risks of foreign contagion. There was much of it in the north-country air.

It was on a visit to Watertown that Cameron met Alice, daughter of Mr Maxford the miller. *When* he actually met her was not really clear in his mind, because in their early days small boys did not pay much attention to small girls, so he was unable to say whether she had been present on the first visit. It had been her brother who had filled Cameron's time and interest with his instant friendship, which they let bloom into madcap antics around town and out into the neighbouring countryside. They went fishing, and found rockfaces to climb. They wheedled good knives out of their fathers and carved all sorts of imaginary weapons from any sticks or branches that suited them, and then fought wars with them. At first, girls did not fit into this, though there came a time when the wars were better if there were someone to fight. Alice and Cameron fought well against each other until the day he discovered they fought better together against others. Then, somehow, those wars were never the same again, and brother Jack slowly became relegated to second fiddle. This took years, of course, so he was quite gracious about it, his own horizons changing in exactly the same way as were Cameron's.

So Alice came back with Cameron on one of those visits, given in wedlock by Mr Maxford. Both Mother and daughter attended, Hilary telling Cameron, that day, that he had for once showed some common sense. Honor, Alice's sister, cried hard as they drew away from the house, for the rumble of War was in the offing, and it was quite possible that the frontier should be closed shut. Alice and Honor were close enough that *their* wars had never seen either one the winner or the loser. It seemed an irony that a marriage band could both bond and cleave in the same moment.

Some time later, through Cameron, Honor met Duncan. As sister to Alice, this was ultimately inevitable, sister and friend coinciding in a visit to the MacNeil home. It was said that she was strong-willed where Alice were less so, though Cameron found his wife to be in full command of him. Still resident on the edge of Watertown, where she looked after her father and brother, she was also teacher to the children of a few merchants who valued script and numeracy as useful skills in their offspring. Duncan immediately professed himself illiterate and enrolled himself at her feet. She wiped them on him for perhaps a couple of months, then someone gave her a dog. His training of it to guard her at all times proved her defences less staunch than she thought, so she found herself caring for *three* men. `Our love's history writ by a canine,' summed up Duncan, one evening, later. Cameron assumed Honor had taught him the word, since he'd never heard Duncan go further than *dog*.

But it was Alice who completely filled Cameron's thoughts. Elder sister, wondrous, loving. *There*, he often told himself, *that is enough, I think, for there are certain moments when even I may blush.*

`Do you keep still, while I put in this last stitch.'

`It burns like hell, and the needle makes it worse.'

`Hush. If Maighster Craig could hear you he'd have you wash your mouth with soap.'

`I'd tell him where to take his soap.'

`Oh, Cameron. You are not meaning that!' Alice was blushing, still bent over his arm as she manoeuvred the needle across the open sides of the cut, bringing the last fold of flesh across the end of the piece of quill. At least her anger at the danger that caused the wound had died. `There, now. It looks clean, so we will hope it heals properly. Any pus will drain out through the end of the quill.' She looked up after biting off the end of the thread, still lightly flushed, hazel eyes finding his heart as they did every time he saw her. She saw his look. `And what are you thinking?'

`Perhaps I shall not say.'

`Perhaps I will make you!' Then, realizing how that could be construed, she blushed again. `Oh, Cameron. The things you make me say.'

He swung her on to my lap, her slender body light against his shoulder. `I love the things you say, just as I love you.'

`Well, that is good then. I should be in an awful pickle if you didn't love me, me with a six-month child.'

`If you giggle so loudly you'll wake him.'

`If he didn't wake from your shouts at the needle, he'll not wake from my giggles. Let me go, you awful man.' But she turned and kissed him soundly on the lips. `My fee.' And she jumped up, laughing openly as she escaped his good arm.

His bad arm lay against the chair, evidence of the narrow escape from the clutches of someone not keen to have him regale anyone with his thoughts. The knife had been large and sharp, and had missed its vital target as Cameron's own pistol cracked the knife's wielder hard against the skull. The latter had folded like a German accordion bereft of air. He'd looked like an Iroquois, but Cameron had been in such a hurry to leave that he hadn't taken in much more than the intent. Duncan had missed it all, ahead with the horses.

Alice seemed to read his thoughts `And where is Duncan?' But she was only confirming her own, given that Duncan had not returned with her husband and that the latter had not brought news any worse than his arm.

`Oh, I should imagine he is with Honor, by now.'

`*Another* reading lesson?' But she gave the true meaning with a further gurgle of laughter.

`Perhaps even now concentrating on her declensions.'

Her resulting hoot woke the other Duncan.

If I am honest, thought Cameron, *I cannot lay my wound at Mr Richard's door. I set myself the problem, and now I wish to see the light of it before I go to him.*

He knew that he would have to discuss it with Cartwright before taking it to Macdonell, because it seemed an issue of trade. And though Mr Cartwright was formally Colonel Cartwright, and it might seem as if Colonel Macdonell played no part in this, any issue of trade which possibly drove the funding of the war across the river was something which would, sooner than later, have to be mentioned to the British Army.

It had been in Cameron's head the moment he'd got away from the Iroquois warrior and the *Periwinkle*. *Let me consider it thus: a barrel of wheat, at approximately five bushels to the barrel is worth about ten shillings; a barrel of potash, at approximately five hundredweight to the barrel, is worth about ten pounds. Which is the more valuable?*

But first he had to answer the question: *to whom?* For it was that which determined value - if no-one bid for a product, then that product was nothing more than wasted labour (and whatever other resources were used to produce it). He had not worked on his father's own farm for many seasons without understanding that while today one may wish (for reasons of survival) to make hay to feed his cattle in winter, tomorrow one might consider a better opportunity that of killing a pig and rendering its fat. The army was hungry for pork.

But he also had to consider this: the army is hungry for pork while it fights a war. When that war is over, will pork be as valuable as wheat or potash?,

The war had driven up the price of everything. When it began, almost two years before, the army knew that there was not enough money in the local economy to finance military expenditures. So it had issued army bills to the value of about £250,000. Now there was almost £1.5 million circulating, a great deal of money by anyone's calculus, and profit was now more easily come by than at any time since the first settlements thirty years before. And, at the moment, there was no end to this war in sight.

But, he thought, while there is easy money in the short term, it would be an imprudent man who gambled his future livelihood on war profit alone. *And that is why I have set myself this problem, because I think I have stumbled on a scheme, and I am extremely worried by it.*

'Two things, sir', he was in front of Mr Richard again.

'As ordered, accompanied by Lieutenant MacLeish, I crossed the river. we arranged for two horses at Old Leggett's, and slowly made our way west. We kept to the edge of the main west-east trade road. We saw the occasional small trader and peddler, but on the whole the road was quiet. On the morning of the 7th, we heard a considerable commotion on the roadway (you will remember, sir, that we had camped a little way off it, to avoid a night surprise). Lt MacLeish, who was on watch, woke me, and we moved quietly to the edge of the road, watching for scouts in the bush. We saw several wagons, heavily loaded, drawn by oxen, moving in the direction of Ogdensburg. We let them pass, and, about fifteen minutes later, followed at some distance. Closing on the edge of town, we decided to split up, and I followed the caravan, leaving Lt MacLeish in the bush with the horses. We agreed that I would rendezvous with him no later than two hours later.'

'What was on the wagons?'

'They were loaded with barrels, sir.'

'You could not tell their contents?'

'They were mostly shielded from the rain with canvas, sir. But the ruts left by the wagons left no doubt that they were heavy.'

'Meat, then? Pork - going downriver?'

'Perhaps, sir. I cannot be certain.'

'And then?'

'They went to the dock, sir. Straight aboard ship.'

'A ship was waiting?'

'Yes, sir. The *Periwinkle*'

'But......., but that's a Navy vessel. And she went downriver two days ago.'

'Yes, sir.'

'Trading on the American side of the river!'

'Apparently so, sir.'

'Then she'd better not be shipping pork to Montreal - we can't get enough of it here. That could be construed treasonable.'

'That's what I thought, sir.'

'Perhaps not pork then?'

'Perhaps not, sir. I could not be certain.'

'But not wheat? Flour?'

'The barrels looked too heavy for that, sir.'

'Hmm. A mystery.'

'That's what I thought, sir.'

'Yes, MacNeil, so what did you then?

'Tried to get closer, sir. To see whether I could recognize a face.'

'And did you? Recognize anyone? Apart from that damned Master of the *Periwinkle*?'

'No, sir, not at that time. Though someone must have recognized me, for the shout went up, and I had to get away. Whatever they were carrying, they didn't want me to know about it.' I held up my wounded arm. 'But I managed to reach Lt MacLeish and after a visit to Glasgie, we retraced our steps across the river. But not before we ran into a Dragoon.' Who had been aboard the Periwinkle, he thought.

'Hmm. Well, see what the Colonel thinks. Doesn't smell too good that, does it?' But he was focussed on the barrels alone,

'Don't think it does, sir, no.'

And a bushel of wheat weighs about 60 lb, so a barrel of flour was going to weigh about three hundredweight. He had hefted barrels himself, and knew the difference in motion, or in the creak of the slings, between three and five hundredweight. It had all looked like potash. And at £10 a barrel, there had been a lot of money in those wagons. And somebody had not wanted him to know.

'Oh, and Leggett may now be compromised.' But if he heard, Mr Richard ignored him, much to his later cost.

The Dragoon Captain presented a problem. It seemed he had *carte blanche* to do whatever he wanted in the north country. As Foster's nephew, no-one was going to say *no* to him, and it seemed he had already worked himself into Macdonnell's good graces. Cameron considered it annoying rather than unfair that he had to take him into account.

The Dragoons were nothing but a nuisance to any scout, but they had particular knowledge that Cameron wished they not have: the location of that first link in the chain. Old Leggett. But he thought that if they had found a way to circumvent the King's Orders when it came to trade, that perhaps they would be too busy to think about anything *else*.

Cameron recalled that first sighting, aboard the *Periwinkle*; the Dragoon Captain had seemed in command of the situation, getting the barrels aboard and out of sight as quickly as possible. Cameron had watched as two loads had been swung aboard, but he knew not how many had followed, he'd been otherwise occupied after that shout. He'd

seen more headed in the same direction when he'd been caught by the Captain himself
on that patrol, and now that he thought about it, he wondered whether the Dragoon
Captain hadn't been on the lookout for barrels rather than having anything to do with
Glasgie and cannonballs.

He had no way of knowing whether he had stumbled on a racket or not, but he knew
that a war hid a lot of other goings-on, and that this could possibly be one of them.

But the Dragoon Captain had no honour (he was actually not aware of this even though
his uncle's position had been drilled into him; it was a concept foreign to him). He lied
to his uncle and his agent as he lied to everyone else; only his men had seen through his
bluster and were close to not taking any more. They thought him common, as, were the
truth known, did his uncle, but the latter overlooked a lot for his sister. The Colonel
across the river was having second thoughts, too.

He kept the potash in an old warehouse. Or rather, he accumulated it there, as he had
no say in how long the King's ships would wait for it, nor how much they would carry at
a time. *About half a load, say up to 40 barrels* he had been told, when he had asked. So 40
it was, and he thought he'd clear at least £160 a trip. At least ten trips,he thought. After
all, he was only sending it to Montreal; after that it would be forwarded God knew
where. The demand was such he made £200 the first time.

He whittled the sticks himself.

'What are those for, then?' asked one of his men.

'Just to put a smile on someones' face,' he said.

His fellow Dragoon thought him crazy, just as he had no inkling of where the
apostrophe should go. The word was singular, but he might have paid attention had he
realized the usage was plural. But he was never advised of plans by the Captain, anyway,
so another unexplained event was not uncommon.

Then the Captain said 'Right, saddle up, then' and all knew that there was some work to
be done. They didn't know whether they'd enjoy it, or not.

They headed first upriver. They left their horses at a farm known to them and crossed to
the island. 'This is where they meet' said the Captain, who'd picked the whisper up at
dinner. He didn't understand that open conversation had it's limits.

None of his men knew what he was talking about, but knew he'd been over the river, so assumed he'd picked up something when someone talked.

'Off the path!' whispered the Captain. Until then he had been looking around desultorily, but the sound of some steps on the path galvanized him into action.

The knife was in Duncan's belly before the other Dragoons could move, more luck than anything else because he would have killed whoever came along that track. He dragged the knife out slowly, making the wound as wide as possible. Duncan slumped to the ground. He smiled. 'Fortune is ours today. The right one came first.'

'One thing before we go. No, perhaps two.'

It was actually three. He proceeded to stretch Duncan's mouth wide so the stick fitted, and pulled some of his entrails out. He looped them over a tree branch. Then he scalped him.

'Now, back to the horses.'

He was followed without a word. Most were trying to keep the last meal down, and all knew where he was heading next. He had mentioned the chain that had to be demolished.

By the time the chain had but one link to break, he called a halt to the day's activities. He had got everyone to speak before bringing closure of the final kind and his men knew where he was headed tomorrow. What he had to gauge was whether his men were up to the task, or if he'd be going alone.

Shriek

What caught Cameron was his intent to press on with his mission even though Duncan had been killed. Duncan died on Canadian soil, and there was a possibility that it had been a random act of violence - a lone stroke of vengeance of a disgruntled native warrior, perhaps. But border scouting brought its own risks, and Cameron was aware that other possibilities also existed. By 1814 the naval race for Lake Ontario had apparently become an obsession, and any act which interfered with achieving that goal would have been dealt with severely. His writing rang with both that risk and his own terror at the thought that he (now that Duncan was dead) had been compromised; the shape of the waiting noose shadowed every page.

Secrets in war are not secrets unless they are known by few. For Duncan and I knew our lives were worth not a whit more than the effort they would put into finding us, were it to be known that we already had the lie of their land. And Duncan was playing the ultimate folly, because he had Honor compromised, though it was not until he understood how much did he love her that he saw what this might mean in price. Oh, our poor Honor!

But I am ahead of myself, because you know not that I left Duncan, colder than he in my anger, and went on to wreak the havoc that we had planned, and I knowing not, in that moment, that I made myself the pawn in a complex game of chess. That horrid second smile, harder this than Duncan's, for the body was already stiff, and no means of calming that agony until the rigor should pass. Old Leggett, caught in a calumny not of his own, but made to pay anyway. And just for the hiding of our boat and the loan of his horses.

You must understand that not all is black and white between the two sides of this border. Even Gildersleeve, that staunch American patriot, would be the first to admit that his forebear's position as King's cup-bearer, even though he speaks of Henry and Richard, and not of George, causes pride where the Revolution allows it not. And we are as susceptible to it as they, for more than one American farmer, selling produce to our merchants, has had his heels cooled in the stocks until he was disabused of the message he thought to sell at home. Lucky they are, to escape hanging. Perhaps not so, I.

And so, as I left Old Leggett, with nothing to be done for him, I knew for certain that this night was to turn the worse yet. For you build a chain from the end, and if Old Leggett, the second link, had let go this earth shortly after Duncan, it were probable that I should find the same smile on Samuel. And then on Jeremiah, And then..., oh, my poor Honor!

But, before I tell you of how that night brought me to understand what the Lord means by darkness, it is proper that I tell you why my Captain Popham did what he did even if I knew not why, then.

I make much of guns and three-deckers. Perhaps this is the simple farm boy in me, used only, before this began, to shooting squirrels with my musket. At least my father allowed this frivolous use of powder, precious as it is, and perhaps not able to afford it, but he saw the value of a skilled shot, and in truth it is a skill that I have boasted at the Fair. And so I saw that the American long guns, shot skilfully, could do far more damage to our fleet, than double the number of our guns shot blindly at their's. So Duncan and I, in the King's Service, had it given to us, not only to see what long guns were put on Eckford's forty-day ships, but to find out from whence they came. And so it came to Popham, Yeo's man, it was said by my lips directly, that Melancthon Woolsey, Chauncey's man, was trailing thirty-four guns from Oswego, to put into the heart of the fleet which would face ours in the season of 1814. And Duncan and I, it really matters not who, also had the whisper that there was not more than a small guard party to the whole convoy. But Popham apparently had heard it from me.

Our Commodore Yeo was filled with the fire that he had perhaps shown off Cayenne, before he took up with St Benedict, seeing an advantage being given to him, for he was worried that his blockade of Sackets Harbor by the two ships the Prince Regent and the Princess Charlotte could end if better guns were to get his range. And better were what the whispers said. Better than any gun we'd seen in the last year, time during which we had built this chain, and used it time and again.

Samuel was not where we had agreed to meet, and responded not to any signal of mine. But nearby I found the simple device which he had left which said that Jeremiah was informed and waiting. I cannot speak of the dread which filled me on not finding him there, device or no, but there was no stopping this now, only a race to the end, so that if I had to pass that final word to Popham it would be within the limits we had set for the foray, and he would withdraw.

Death carries a smell. Not as simple as a scent of fresh blood, nor as pungent as the stink of rot, both of which are just stages of corruption. I talk of death, that departure of the soul from the body, after which the earthly cage is irrelevant to memory, even though we bestow rights upon it in honour of the departed. The smell of death is something closer to a shriek, the tearing of the fabric that makes us human, even if war proves we behave like animals.

So understand that as I neared Jeremiah's place, with Samuel's forked stick in my hand, I smelt death as it is inhumanely brought to pass. More than his device, the stick was a talisman, I had hoped, for as evidence that Samuel had been and gone, perhaps because he himself had been worried, it had served its purpose; if I carried it with me I thought perhaps I would be able to return it to his hand and joke about my concern, finding that it had kept him safe. But when I came to that cabin less than two miles distant from Sackets Harbor, I had no doubt that Jeremiah, at least, would be unconcerned about whether I had brought Samuel's device or not. I knew that he was dead, and that as Samuel's device, in a forked stick we'd chosen poorly.

But I was unprepared for what I found, strung up like a shot stag in fall. For it was Samuel's face that greeted me, stretched in that gaping smile, though not in pleasure at the full weight of his body pulling his thumbs out of their sockets, nor at the bow-shots that riddled him like some giant porcupine. And if that were not bad enough, the slow give in the twist of the rope span him like a long-clock weight, replacing his head with Jeremiah's feet, and his feet with Jeremiah's head. Though if the bodies were inverted in reference to each other, the smiles had been carefully tended to greet me in common plane.

The presence of death is silence. One does not count the night sounds, which are no more than nature's breath. So I both smelt and heard those deaths, sure that I was alone with what were my friends because this thing was not done yet, and my death was still some way down this path. I was being led by my own certainty, a thin cord of reason in this frayed and flayed mind of mine, that there was to be a message beyond mere loss of life. Though to be able to look upon these corpses and describe it as mere loss of life, was because I knew who was next. One does not equate the taking of a man's life with the taking of a woman's.

Why were these people dead? It was a terrible question, with an answer most likely worse. But secrecy had been a maxim we had insisted upon in our fight with Sackets Harbor, because there is little humour in war, and none of us wanted another's death as the ultimate joke upon his head. And Duncan and I had worked, from the moment it became clear that Sackets' slipways would be the key to the game in Upper Canada, to establish our sources as untainted and unquestionable. Not the people who loudly voiced their displeasure over their southern cousins' pressure to engage in war, yet who left the account payable to and by those who traded across lake and river; no, rather those who sought quietly to defuse the keg that others lit, and people, above all, whom we knew.

103

So they were killed because we knew them. And I knew that, one way or another, they were always to die, and that, had I reached Shovel Island first, it would be Duncan here now. Perhaps it were the only small mercy permitted that night that he was not, for there still was Honor.

I am plagued by dreams. Dreams of dinner and women. This time I recognize my partner as Nancy. I do not talk to her of Peru, but Peru lurks as a third presence throughout everything.

We are in a restaurant. Often she leans forward to listen very carefully to something I say, and my eyes slip to the shadows deep inside the lip of her bodice. Her slender throat is wrapped with a thin golden chain which itself disappears into those shadows. Her eyes, when mine come up to meet them, say nothing specific, and though she relaxes somehow the shadows become vibrant, dynamic, urgent. A finger wraps itself around the chain, and raises and lowers it at regular intervals. I start to think of the chain as a flag halliard, raising a fluttering standard to the top of an elegant flagpole, but it very quickly becomes the image of a wellrope, something suspended on it in the shadows, nothing like a bucket.

I very quickly know what I want, and there is not a single question in my mind as to whether it is a wise decision. If the question ever existed, from the moment I meet her in my dream it is one stillborn, that stillbirth somehow catalysed by all that is boiling within me. But if she reads my need in eyes that perhaps too easily speak of deeper distress, it is not one of us in particular who leads us back to my room. There, I tie myself on the end of that wellrope, and plunge for all my life into the depths she offers. At some moment all physical points of reference disappear into a single enveloping urgency, where nothing matters but the ability to give and take all in the same blinding instant.

But, through my own fault, I am devoured, as the mantis or spider is wont to devour her mate. No telling myself that the male half of the highest order of mammalian life is no less fragile when the female is ripe did anything to lessen the void that was now black before me, because she took me during a rage, and I was powerless, at the moment she showed herself, to stop. Then she was gone, in five minutes.

When I awake, I feel a dreadful loss. For I am sapped as if life itself has been taken, as if she knew, in my dream, that it was the easiest stroke possible, the man under her unable even to gain his knees from his previous punishment.

How does a man become sure that God has deserted him? There may be many ways, to none of which Maighster Craig would admit, extolling as he does every Sunday from that pulpit we so carefully built him that God is always with every one of us. But that deadly smile took, for many minutes, all belief away. For the pain recently felt by the man before me had to be the devil's own mockery, the rictus of that arched back, the smile whittled into that harrowed face, the exposed entrails.

After the dream sleep would not come back immediately, so I hoped that Cameron's words would be my solace, for I found that my bed felt empty and I did not want it so. Though there was little in any of Cameron's writing that spoke to solace, because it was a tale from a man perhaps beyond despair.

But this was not the first time I'd read everything that he had to say, and it was perhaps little short of justice that the diary opened where it did. This time, though, his words pierced the dusty surface of that almost two hundred year-old layer of forgotten memory and forced themselves into my brain as exactly the same sense of dreadful loss that I felt. For in Peru, as in the dream, I had been sapped as if *my* life had been taken.

And so I became deadly afraid, because it was a chain that Duncan and I had built over many months, several links to it, essential to that night, and I was being clearly shewn that we had worked for naught.

But in my case, in that first punishment, there had been no smile of any form left on my hosts' faces, the torn throats no longer possible witness to any happiness at all. I put his words away, and turned the light out, forcing myself to endure the dark and whatever images it might bring. I had no right to feel anything good. But I wondered what it was in me that, in my dream, made Nancy, a woman I was only just getting to know, a figure of so much malice.

Sleep had not come, so I'd, once more, taken recourse in Cameron's world. I read again his final words. *And so I commend to God and the future my fellowes of the King's Border Scouts, and particularly John Greaves, Abel Lattimore, Henry Anderson, William Horrocks and Phillip Whittaker. They may see me depart this earth; I, not so, they.*

Goodbye, my Alice. And God forgive me.

The signature was no less crisp and firm than the rest of his writing, but those last words must have been written very shortly before dawn on the day he was hanged for the pages before suggested he slept not at all that last night. If his story as a whole had caused him trouble in its writing there was no sign, no wavering, in that elegant almost eighteenth-century hand. Anger there certainly was, over the deaths of Duncan and Honor, the other members of his chain, and all those slaughtered in Popham's raid. But, apart from protesting his own innocence, not once did he suggest who had been behind it all; not once did he rail against forces of injustice. I had no doubt that what he had written was completely true: the words rang with truth and, unlike today, honour made the truth important.

He hadn't mentioned his five friends by name before, and I suddenly saw the Border Scouts as bigger than just him and Duncan. But it was obvious, really, given the area in which the Kingston garrison was maintaining a threadbare defence while putting out the image of a sustained and sustainable force. So there were other pairs on equally dangerous assignments, perhaps also suffering the setbacks he and Duncan had faced, returning home wounded and convalescing before the next mission, perhaps not returning at all. And perhaps the Sackets Rangers were no different, just on the opposite side of that colander of a border, but men (and women) of similar commitment, suffering equally.

'Why do you think he mentioned them by name?'

'What do you mean?'

'Cameron mentions five of his friends in the Border Scouts by name. Why? And he quite distinctly says 'particularly', as if there were something special about them.'

'They were probably his close friends, and he wanted that friendship remembered by others.'

'You don't find it strange how he closes that paragraph? That they may see him depart this earth, but he not so, they? Why would he expect to see them die if he were still around?'

David's mind was considerably clearer than mine, which was suffering all the effects of a foreshortened night. 'You can't tell that is specifically what he means. And perhaps they were older than him.'

He took a sip of the coffee in front of him. 'You are not thinking. They wouldn't have hired relicts from 1784 as border scouts. These men would have been the same age as he was.'

He was right, of course. But I felt dull. The lights of the café did little to cheer me up. 'So?'

David looked at me inquisitively. 'Why so obtuse? Didn't you sleep well?'

I put my mind to the task, breast-stroking through the fog. `Sorry. Yes, I do understand what you mean. Tell me what you think.' I signalled the waitress for another coffee.

`I think he put those names in there for a purpose.'

`A signal?'

`That's a good word. Yes, a signal. To someone.'

`To whom?'

`That's the question, isn't it? Who was going to read those diaries?'

`He left them to his father. And Alice.'

`And would his father have been in a position to do anything? If he'd understood the signal? Or would Alice?'

I thought about the other signal I had missed. `No, I doubt it. If Cameron was recently hanged, it would take more than protests from a close relative to move anyone to take a closer look at the case. I think he was looking farther into the future.' *Lo siento mucho, señora.*

`So he had faith that someone would read them, that if there was a particular message implicit in those five names it would be understood.'

`Maighster Craig.'

`What?'

`Maighster Craig, the minister. I've just remembered. There is a note about him in some of the papers. Not in his hand, but in Cameron's father's.' And Cameron's father's words took me even farther back in that ancestral line, where, if I'd almost begun to see Cameron as a brother, the father, too, took form as closer than history made us.

`And what does he say?'

The remaining papers were still in my hotel room, not to hand as we drank coffee at a small round table halfway up Princess St. I'd been given the message by the desk clerk, that David would be there at about ten o'clock if I could make it. He'd mentioned the place before, good Italian pastries to go with the coffee, and the message had been secondhand only because I'd taken the phone off the hook in my desperation to sleep as long as I could if sleep were to come. Recalling Cameron's words and showing David that last page had seemed a simple way to start the day.

`That they'd been given to him well after Cameron's hanging. More than a year, I think.'

I thank Maighster Craig for keeping them safe.

'Why so long?'

'Perhaps the war.'

'He was probably the last man to talk to him.'

'To Cameron?'

'I think Cameron would have wanted absolution of some sort before his death, wouldn't he? He had a wife and child. Surely the minister would have walked those last steps with him.'

'And the diaries would have been put into his hands that last morning. Yes, you're right. So for some reason they stayed in the minister's keeping until being given to Cameron's father.'

'Perhaps they would have been considered very sensitive material if their existence became known. Perhaps the minister was instructed to keep them until he felt it safe to pass them on.'

'Why would they have been safer with him than with Cameron's father? Or wife?'

'It must have been a very emotional time, Alastair. If it were you who had suffered the loss of a brother or husband hanged, and you read something that suggested someone else was the true villain, or at least that the condemned considered it a wrongful hanging, what would you do?'

It required no answer, because one would move heaven and earth to right a suspected miscarriage of justice. Go home, Carlos had said. You are in no condition to do anything about this now. Recover first, and then write about it. Put it in the world's press, so that people really understand. But I was still unable to write about it, still numb, though the coffee was dangerously evocative of coffee shared with Carlos during those few mornings of returning pain. 'Cameron must have had a very strong sense that justice would eventually be brought. He must have known that there was something somewhere that would bring the truth to light. Perhaps he wanted it done when war was no longer a distraction, when people could view the story dispassionately. What a price he paid.'

'In those days, honour was often bought at very high cost. Perhaps Yeo paid some of it.'

'Why Yeo?'

'Yeo must have lost face in Popham's failed attack on Sackets Harbor. Publicly it may have been expedient to move the blame elsewhere. Nothing has ever suggested that Yeo himself was not an honourable man, but if he believed that the decision to send Popham was critically flawed and that some of the blame was his, hanging Cameron made someone else pay for his own mistake. He would not have slept soundly for a long time. But did Cameron's father read the diaries?'

`His are the first notes. But they are no more than a father's cry for a son lost to war. I think he had no reason to believe that Cameron was not guilty. Remember, if the minister said nothing about the diaries for a year or more, he would have lived with the official story long enough for it to be a bitter memory. Perhaps it would have brought more pain to have opened it in the face of still recent events.'

`Then who did first question what had happened?'

`Cameron and Alice's son. Duncan.'

Partners

There was another note at the desk when I got back to the hotel, and I thought it a little odd that it hadn't been Nancy who had left it. Perhaps she, too, was suffering from a lack of sleep.

I phoned immediately, and was put through to a Dean more formal than when we had first met, but this may just have been the distance of the intervening days. `Yes, Mr MacNeil. Thank you for returning my call. Nancy says you've agreed to her proposition, and I was wondering if you could join us for a meeting with Bracehams this evening. We'll probably have dinner.'

So, Nancy had made a commitment on my behalf which was less than truthfully my wish - whenever I had approached the topic she'd skated around it, not letting me come out with a definite `no'. Like Yeo, I recognized a battle lost; unlike Yeo, I had no wish to see Nancy as he'd seen Chauncey - a critical opponent.

Bracehams turned out to be two executives interested in a relaxing evening after a hard business day. Neither one had known my grandfather, the corporate world apparently more fluid than the academic one, and the little talk there was of mechanical engineering suggested that they had even less time for independent inventors.

The Dean had chosen a new steakhouse for the event, and that was perhaps his only correct move of the evening, for Bracehams went for the largest cuts on the menu. Beer followed the earlier beer in the bar while we'd taken time to meet each other, though Nancy stuck to wine.

It didn't take me long to understand how Nancy had planned the evening - apparently according to her own expectations of Bracehams. She sat herself between the two of them and, though not so clothed, put on an act little short of any undressed tool-girl on a garage poster. She was clearly back in a shell, a life-form in a primitive world where subtlety supposedly worked not at all. But she surprised me by the extent to which she pushed herself.

I glanced at the Dean, to see whether he had any inkling of what was going on. On the whole I thought he probably did, though I think he was less interested in the specific and more concerned with general damage control in the event that Nancy went overboard. Perhaps even academic engineers lived closer to the tool-buying stereotype than I'd thought.

When the time came to make the pitch, Nancy held little back. 'Alastair, of course, is a well-known foreign correspondent, and he's agreed to lend his name to our lecture series. So, not only do we have the MacNeil Endowment Fund, which will help us become the leading research group in our field in Canada, but we have the MacNeil Invitational Lectures. Grandfather and grandson in the cause of mechanical engineering. Isn't that right, Alastair?'

I thought the Dean should be exploring this ground, but he seemed content to leave it to Nancy. She clearly thought she controlled her puppet's strings, so I decided on some minor clarification: 'My grandmother left a lot of money to Queen's, but wanted it used for research. In my grandfather's name. The Dean believes that a supporting lecture series will increase Queen's standing still further, and I should like to help him with his vision of a future centre of excellence. I, unfortunately, have no money, so I lend a hand in the search for corporate sponsors.' Nancy looked sulkily at me at my reference to the Dean, and my less-than-purposeful approach. I thought the price fair.

'Alastair is too modest.' Her gaze was brooding and went elsewhere as she spoke. ' His talents bring their own qualities to this series. He will soon be making Kingston his home, and we will ask him to introduce every speaker. Any sponsor associated with us will soon gain wide recognition.'

It was clear that she was on ground that was new to the Dean. He turned to me in surprise. 'I didn't know that, Alastair. That makes it more interesting, doesn't it?'

'I think Nancy is a little ahead of herself. I haven't made any such decision.'

'Oh, but we talked about it last night, Alastair. Don't you remember?' She turned to the each man beside her. 'He's a little shy.'

The coyness was so distant from her extrovertedness of the previous hour that they were both startled. 'Well, it's a great place, Alastair. A fair city,' said Bracehams senior.

`I've never thought any different,' I said. `However, it is not my home, yet, in spite of what Nancy says.'

She became the businesswoman, and the purpose of the evening came again to the fore. `Bracehams has the opportunity of leading the pack. If you can let us know quickly, we will guarantee your name at the head of the list.'

`And how much is this likely to cost us? The guarantee, I mean.' Bracehams senior knew the value of unit cost, and had made a distinct separation between being just *a* sponsor, and being *the* sponsor.

`Well, just a little more, perhaps. Say, ten thousand?'

The Dean blanched a little, perhaps unused to hitting clients for such heady sums.

Bracehams senior chortled. `Tax receipted, of course.'

`Why, yes.' Nancy was earnest in her entreaty.

Even so, Bracehams stayed noncommittal, and the Dean paid the bill, asking after one or two common acquaintances as his own contribution to the end of the conversation. The group made its way to the front door, and Bracehams went to its separate cars.

`Thank you for coming, Alastair. Can you find your own way home?' The Dean took my hand, a little edgy in his movements, and not looking at Nancy. He escaped as quickly as he could.

Nancy forestalled my move to phone for a taxi, and took my arm almost as a gesture of possession of spoils. Suddenly she was as gentle as a new mother. `Did you enjoy the evening? I thought it went quite well.'

I thought quite the opposite, and was almost as sure that Bracehams, apart from the steaks consumed, was glad to go home. `I think you'll need to look at other possibilities to complete your sponsorship.'

`Oh, I doubt it. I just think you'll have to be a little more persuasive.'

She drove into the hotel parking lot. I was suddenly aware that I was standing on another precipice, and that I'd crafted this one even less carefully than the last.

Honor; a name uncommon today, but, then, one that would have helped fulfill all the expectations a man had of a future wife: chaste, respectful, noble. Duncan fell in love with her, and Cameron saw her death as his own dishonour, far more serious that the deaths of the others: *It was her death that will hang me, if that is the outcome of this. For it brought a different emotion to the faces of the Bench. Even in war a woman's passing is to be measured differently, and if the Cause is to hand, then shall he be made to pay.*

It were typical of Duncan that he should fall for a schoolmistress, for he'd been the worst of students, book learning the bane of his natural existence. We were different in this, for I saw what Man wrote in a book as the extension to what he understood of his World; Duncan saw it as taking up the time he would rather spend in it. And by in it I talk of this wondrous bounty of Nature that God wrought here. Water and islands; can there be anything more fine? We thought not.

But Nature has its obverse, just as any of the King's coins. Man it is that has the capacity to wreck all that is wondrous, and here he tore the dual fabric of love and life. But in killing Honor, he made his own victory base. I can only thank God that Duncan did not know.

In sleep they had destroyed her peace. She was presented to me in the folds of a hammock, the blood on the deck underfoot issue of a monstrous wound made where blood would otherwise have flowed in birthing. Her bare breasts mocked me. And again, that smile, stretched between cheeks that had been so fair, but which now were no more than any harlot's creased and pitted flesh. That smile cackled its hideous laughter at me.

In a second I knew that this were a ship that should never float, unless it were to take Honor to Duncan. But as I scrabbled in my tunic for tinder and flint, wanting beyond all else an instantly miraculous inferno, more arms than I could resist took hold of me, and pressed me against the gundeck bulkhead. And, in that instant, all my case was lost.

They had calculated well. I had gone undisturbed from Jeremiah's woodland cabin to the USS Superior on her stocks on the slip. I came to her from the water, sculling the deep shadows in Honor's own skiff. Watch fires burned onshore, casting their glow inland, though an imagined warmth of visibility scorched my face. I came to spike what guns she may have had on board, expecting Popham, towards Oswego, to finish the rest. The time it would take the gunsmith to rebore the guns' taper holes was clear water for Yeo; Chauncey would keep to his dockyard bed until it were done. But I was unable to spike even the one, and not only because Honor was my welcome near Superior's very gunport that gave me entry.

There was no fear of fire here, the timber too green to burn, and my effort with tinder and flint would have been no more than the dream I had wished for Honor's journey. Smoking brands appeared once they had me fast, and, thrust into my face, brought the identification they had expected.

Then they took me and made me watch Popham's own capture.

It became a matter of court record that I was brought to Kingston under an agreement of truce. Why this? It takes little to see that my captors wished Popham's loss to be blamed on a traitor rather than on themselves, for it were far better to turn the anger of that loss inward and use it to stretch the neck of one man, than to risk further imprudence from the very foe they feared. Though I am the only one to see it, for I can get it through no-one's head that had I wished to be the traitor I am accused of being, Honor's final greeting served me none. I should not have been anywhere near that ship.

Alice, no matter what they say, I killed not your sister.

`Duncan had a son's anger at the loss of a father he'd hardly known. I don't know what age he was when Alice or his grandfather showed him the diaries for the first time, but proving his father's innocence became an obsession. Perhaps even the minister spoke to him. I should imagine that Cameron left some specific words for his son.'

The breakfast room, really an extension of the kitchen, looked out onto the back garden and the river beyond. The early sun came in over Penny's right shoulder and brought a halo into her golden hair. She was concentrating on her toast, but examining the glint of sunlight in the dollop of strawberry jam on her right index finger. She revolved it from side to side.

We'd not finished our coffee conversation, that morning two days before. Some alumni were coming to town, and David had left at a brisk walk for the campus. But he had offered breakfast, and as his interest sharpened my thoughts generally (and, I had thought, more so if sleep continued to be sparse), I had accepted. Now, I needed David to help me keep my thoughts on Cameron; Penny needed no help to keep hers on strawberry jam.

`But if Alice was Honor's sister, I wonder if she ever believed Cameron.' Angie had a sister's doubts, not knowing what depth of love Alice might have held for her husband. Penny carefully evaded her attempt to wipe that finger clean of jam.

I'd unrolled the contorted family tree for them, finally exposing that extra bond that brought Cameron and Duncan closer. It must also have been a bond that wrought emotional havoc at a time when Alice needed to believe completely in Cameron, and Cameron needed her to believe in his innocence. But I had no doubts: *I believe you, Cameron, but as it was not you, then who was it?* `I think so. That would have been essential to son Duncan's own conviction.'

David looked through the steam rising off his coffee. `What did son Duncan achieve? Did he manage to change public perception of Cameron's guilt?'

`No. And it seems to have been his obsession that got in the way. He wasn't able to construct a rational argument.'

Angie was cutting Penny's second piece of toast in half for her. `I should think it must have been very hard for him to collect any evidence. Even we don't know what really happened.' Then she looked at me. `Do we?'

`The rest of the papers, over the subsequent generations, speculate on many things. From Duncan the elder having somehow given the game away, or Honor letting something slip, to the possibility that Yeo made a deal with the devil.'

Angie frowned. `What do you mean?'

`That Cameron was made the scapegoat for Yeo's failure.'

David shook his head. `But that wouldn't account for the five deaths.'

`I've found nothing other than Cameron's own words that speak to those deaths.'

`But I thought those were what the Americans sent him back to pay for.' Angie continued to frown.

`Popham's failure is a known fact. But the deaths of the other four were not mentioned in any report Chauncey's office made to Yeo. Cameron was sent back as having betrayed Britain. Our hanging him was the dividend they wanted.'

`They didn't give any of the Canadian Volunteers the same treatment?'

`Not that I know of.'

David, the historian, showed his knowledge. `It was unlikely that they played individually important roles on a scale like this. Naval control of the two lower Lakes was assumed to be the key to an American victory; sometimes we find that hard to comprehend today. They would have wanted Yeo to know the depths of his failure; Cameron's return was a gambit in the spring campaign.' It began to sound a little like how I imagined one of his lectures would be. `It was the act, not so much the man.'

I nodded. `So son Duncan was unable to find any evidence of effort to look into Cameron's story. The loss of Popham's men was enough to call for the rope, elder Duncan they ignored, and no-one thought that there might be anything else to consider. Remember, Cameron presented little defence.' *He, I fear, is more concerned for his wig.*

`Poor man.' The very real suffering Cameron's last weeks would have brought him weighed in Angie's words.

Penny's arms, free of toast, crept around my neck from behind. `Poor Aster.' So I made a lightning grab for her right hand. `Um, delicious.' And she ran laughing from the kitchen, wiping her wet finger on her pants as she went.

Neil Thomas

Dinners

The Angela who responded to my dinner invitation was a woman who had taken care with her appearance: soft wool dress for a cool fall evening, silk scarf, and shoes to sit (or dance) in rather than for walking. Her early mood was gay, someone doing something uncommon, and happy to be out of the house. We drove east, along the old King's Highway, and found a restaurant thirty minutes distant which was not overcrowded. The main criterion had been lack of parking for tourist buses, followed by a hint in the name which suggested that an old redbrick pile could house interesting food.

There are still some restauranteurs who understand the value of small rooms, small tables, and lighting which keeps your sight within a very small radius. It allows you to concentrate on your food, and on the person with you. A decent menu and moderate wines are then enough, because it is the whole that counts. Slowly, by the time we'd reviewed what was on offer from the kitchen and cellar, I began to feel that everything had been lined up for us, balm for me at least.

`Penny says hi.'

`Did she want to come?'

`At first. But Dad promised her double stories at bedtime, so she agreed to an early night.'

`Will you tell me about her?'

Angela buried her nose in her wineglass, and I thought I'd made a very early mistake, but then I saw she was thinking. Her finger traced a pattern in the tablecloth.

`I lived with someone for a period. Penny was the result.' It still hurt, I could see, so there could be no more questions. There was silence and I thought her statement had ended the conversation. Her gaiety had gone. But she hadn't finished. `I made the mistake of getting involved at work. He saw me as an easy target; I saw him as my other half. By the time I found out, I was already pregnant. When he found that out, he dropped me flat.' She breathed in, a slight tremor in her breath. `He asked for a transfer, and I found out about it through office gossip.'

`Did he go?'

She smiled wryly. `I spoke to my Department Head. We agreed that it didn't seem fair that he should go immediately. He had to wait until Penny was born. Not that we stayed together during that period. But he saw me every day at the station, and as everyone else knew who the father was, he had a rough time.' She was quiet a moment. `I think he's in Cobalt, now. They were glad to get him, a big-city-trained policeman'.

`You don't see him?'

`He bargained away his rights. And I have no wish to see him. Penny never has.'

`She seems well for it.'

`Thank you. I don't think I could bear it if people thought otherwise. It was one of the reasons I moved in with Dad. He provides another permanent presence in her life, and they get on well together. Of course, she fills a gap for him, too.'

It was time for a silence. But thoughts take advantage of silence, and it was easy for them to cluster in that part of the brain that displays them to the world as expression. Angie must have been looking at me more closely than I thought: `Tell me about your trouble. Why does it affect you so deeply?' Then, because I was startled and she thought that I might not have understood: `No, not Cameron; Peru.'

As the one question I didn't want to answer it was perfect. The waitress brought a soup while I still looked for a way out, but there was a creeping understanding in me that I would have to talk about it, and that if anyone were to hear the words it should be Angela.

So I spoke the dream; the first.

`Desert and coffee?'

The quiet words from the waitress must have been the first spoken at that table for more than a minute. Angela's hand had stopped the flow of dreadful images across my mind, a touch of warmth creeping into a gray cold flickering cinema of the underworld, climbing up from the back of my hand and into the synapses of present thought. I raised my head and looked at her, wondering what she thought about a soul stripped bare.

`But why is the ideological struggle so bloody?'

`Simply put, ideology is obsession. When people become obsessed they become irresponsible.' I could feel my anger now, what had been done to these people and in the name of the *patria*, that godlike concept of nationhood that swelled the breasts of those in power until it reached their heads and drove them off the throne of decency. And once decency was gone, it was lost to all subsequent generations, because all the subsequent sons of the *tierra* knew was loss and vengeance and how to stick the knife in, in order to steal something back. Knives had been stuck into these people for centuries, a shorter blade sometimes the only respite. They had always been the victims.

The waitress brought whatever it was we'd ordered, and we pushed it around our plates a little.

`But surely not the military.' Angela found that part of it hard to believe, that a uniform did not automatically make its wearer a public servant - protector, in this case, of the very little that these people had.

`Politics will distort reasonable behaviour to the point where it reverts to something worse than the jungle.' *Where there is gain, there will you find greed; where there is greed, God be your protector.* It had been the moment when Cameron had understood. `The man's wife put it more simply, in terms more relevant to her. "They are but men, *señor*, to whom guns and knives are given for killing. They are expected to be the way they are."'

`Were they glad to see you leave?'

I, the coward, took the easy way out, still unable to cope with that final image. `It was too dark, and I couldn't tell.' Because tell I still couldn't, and admit that I'd orchestrated their deaths before both Man and God. Instead, I paid the bill, and we left.

The weather turned into an early winter lesson, no snow, but everything else. I stayed in the hotel all day, reading, transcribing. Grandmother was very close, part of the room's warmth.

In the early evening the phone rang, but when I answered it no-one responded. I hung up abstractedly, little disturbed from my book. The wind was still blowing hard outside, the rain hard enough to strip the maples further along the road of their leaves. It was a night to stay at home. But after another half hour, perversely, I decided to go out and feel the rain on my face.

There were not many people on Princess St, and my walk up it became a series of encounters with the wind, block by block blasting into my left ear, channelled along the cross streets. After several it left my cheek stinging. The warmth of the small Asian cafe brought a heightened burn.

The proprietor was glad of a customer, and delivered both the menu and my selection very quickly. He'd been generous with the spices, and I lost myself somewhere between the lime-based tang of the noodles and the crispness of the beer. Together they brought a resurging sense of well-being, and, for a moment, I felt as if I were beginning to recover. Somewhere outside the alarm of a passing fire-truck fluted on the flows of the wind.

I had a second beer once the noodles were gone, and it brought reflection, that inward review of whatever is piled up in the mind. My particular pile started taking on some order, and I recognized that my feeling of recovery was partially true, that distance was lending shape to some events so that I could see them and cope with them better. My guilt was no less, but I was able to put it into terms relative to that current war as a whole. It was not the watershed that dragging everything to the surface would finally be, but there was a sense that I would eventually see that I had done, or would finally have done, once the story was written, some of what I could to make amends.

I wandered elsewhere, seeing the scars of something else, doubting that I'd yet climbed out of the last hole I'd dug for myself. I count, on the fingers of about three hands, the number of women I've taken to dinner in whom I've had more interest than purely professional. But that has sunk to a hand and a half by the time dinner was over and I'd heard about motivation and want, not necessarily in those terms, but definitely as elements of the main message. To be fair, I think the reverse is true, and I have bored the ears off more than half, trying to put into words my own message, and finding blank looks when anything of a competing, professional commitment to a relationship shouldered its way into the conversation. Only two fingers count when I consider relationships, and none if I think of permanence.

Now, I'd had two dinners, as different from each other as they could possibly be. The first, with Bracehams *et al*. The second, had been part of a flow through David, a progression of events that had made me share something of myself with Angela. We had explored each other from different vantages, and I have no doubt she found me badly cracked, most of my paint blistered; she, I found abandoned on a ledge, surviving on what she had been left, glad though for the love she had able both to create and to give.

Perhaps the images of the second dream were correct - that the moment had pushed all my previous shifting images of tension, death and blame into some hidden corner so that there would seem no risk to dreaming it. Indeed, I had not told Nancy my story, and quickly understood that my first dream should remain an unexplained nightmare, recurring though it was. I feared that it would be laughed at.

As I sorted through these thoughts, a greater one began to form in my mind. It did not come simply, because it had already taken days to develop this far. But I sensed Grandmother's hand in this. Grief at her loss had been subsumed into the greater sorrow for the results of my other, disastrous actions, and apart from the reason for those early tears observed by Lacroix, I had not tried much to give order to the elements of my distress. Now, something else was emerging, though it was still unformed - try as I might, it would not come further.

The last drops of beer were warm, no continuing catalyst to this process of understanding. The mind went back to its muddle, so I paid the check and waited for the change.

It was a full-blooded storm coursing across the river front when I got back to the hotel, and I expect the officials marshalling people away from the hotel were glad of it, because it would do something to keep down some of the flames. Three trucks, lights flashing but sirens silent, were ranged around the forecourt, and streams of water poured from the hoses into upper level windows. The fire looked as though it had taken a whole floor, and was spreading to the one above. I counted the windows up from the ground, confirming the fear felt when I'd first seen the reflection of a red, pulsing light in the windows of another restaurant, away on the opposite corner.

Angie had been there before me, the police station only a block away, and her turn to work late. She came out of the mass of people and stood beside me. There was a slight tremor in her voice. `I'm glad to have found you.'

`I was out having dinner.'

`You were the only one of your floor not accounted for.'

`Sorry.' And I was, because it was clear that there was not much left of my room, and there would be even less of its contents. The second bed had still been covered in papers.

`It spread very fast.'

`What started it?'

`Nobody's sure. But the management is surprised that the sprinkler system didn't control it.'

`It was working?'

`Oh yes. All the controls were functioning. It got too hot, too fast.'

David was very quickly forthcoming with a brandy. Penny was fast asleep, it being a work day, so only the three of us sat in those chairs. But the brandy did very little for a different anger, that extended contact with my family now lost, in its original handwritten form anyway. At least nothing had been unread.

`You'll stay here, Alastair. I'll fix you a bed in a while.'

`You're very kind. Thank you.'

`Not at all.' David shook his head. `And don't think about moving out for now.'

`No,' I protested. `It wasn't much. I travel very lightly.'

`That's got nothing to do with it. I have few opportunities to have guests, now. It will be a pleasure for me to have you here.'

Most of his friends would be married, most still with spouses. I knew it would be hard for him to entertain them, with the most important place at the table empty. `Thank you.'

`That's settled, then.'

Angie stirred, yawning. `I'm sorry. Reaction, I think. I was worried sick for a while.' Her face was still white.

David poured us all some more brandy. `I'll make some sandwiches.'

Angie said nothing as he left. David had lit a fire against the storm, and the light from the burning logs flickered on eyes that stared into their middle. Then, `You hadn't left your key.'

`No. It was in my pocket. An old habit.'

`I didn't know. You understand?'

`Yes.'

She was reliving her fear, letting it out. Far better than I ever had been able to. `It was impossible to get onto the floor, let alone into your room. They asked me if you were a smoker.'

`No.' But I didn't mean that I wasn't a smoker. `Don't think about it.'

She was crying now. `It was an inferno before anyone could get there to check it. I really thought you were gone.'

She was still staring into the fire, so didn't see my twisted smile. `I seem to be living a charmed life.'

David brought in a tray, a large plate of sandwiches covering most of it. We sat there working our way through smoked salmon between something multi-grained; some white wine went with it. Another log went on the fire. `What will you do now?'

`Nothing has changed, David. I started something I want to see finished; there is still some work to do.'

`But I thought you'd lost everything in the fire.'

I went out into the hallway and brought the small black shoulderbag that had been with me all afternoon. Out came my small laptop, a file of drawings, and three faded blue and gold notebooks. The drawings included Grandfather's cams and bearings, but there were also industrial flowcharts of some sort, and I had wondered whether they described processes already installed, or other things that he'd worked on but left unfinished. They looked like fluid transport systems, lines connected by valves, either joining or separating flows. My knowledge of engineering draughtsmanship was insufficient to tell in which direction things went, and Grandfather's notes at each level of the system, appearing as labels for each line, did not help. Each label was nothing but zeros and ones, and the occasional comma or dash. I'd taken them to dinner with me, wanting to study them some more, but other thoughts had taken command and I'd left them untouched. `I had finished transcribing the other papers today. These,' and I indicated Cameron's diaries, `are never left anywhere.' *For I am you, Cameron, and you are me.*

David left Angie and me to see the fire die down. Angie found some Segovia, and we listened to his nimble old fingers pick their way through several Spanish folksongs, the music far more eloquent for the moment than any words of mine. After a while, the firelight dimmer, Angie moved from her chair and sat on the floor with her back against the front of mine, her head leaning sideways against my thigh. My hand moved into her hair, combing gently, and then slid down to her neck. There it spent an half hour taking all the tension out, leaving me, at least, with a lot to think about, in my separate bed.

Neil Thomas

Prices

Ancestral lines can be as if rule-drawn, or as intricate as a sinnet. The fact that I was still a MacNeil, direct descendant of Cameron, when it was my father who was Grandmother's son, owed itself to earlier deaths, for mother was Grandfather's daughter, and there was no consanguinity between children made brother and sister by a second marriage. Even so, they had not tried to sanctify their union locally, recognizing the reaction it would have brought. They took themselves out of the community they felt had brought them the unhappiness of the first parental deaths, never able to see that second conjunction as the blessing that life occasionally bestows on those whom death has left behind, if not untouched. Knowing how Grandmother loved Grandfather may have been part of the trouble, as it was principally my mother's jealous reaction to their evident joy that snared my father the way it did.

So, while I was born in wedlock, I came into this world constrained within very short bounds of love, leaving them only when I choked on pipesmoke, or heard different stories told uncomplainingly at bedtime in that old limestone house.

`Genealogy,' said David, `is the study of bodies past. Not a literal exhumation, of course. And therefore a lot less smelly.' He was enjoying his academic's humour. `But it may help.'

But I'd already got Cameron's family tree well drawn, at least, my line of descent from him, and thought that there was little help there. I told him so.

`No. Not your family. I'm thinking again of the five names finally mentioned. There is something there that intrigues me.' He'd seen them before breakfast, up early and perusing Cameron's copperplate hand as I came out of the land of sleep. Apparently he'd started at the back and worked forwards, interested, first, in capturing the effect of a known and coming death.

`A signal,' said Angie.

`Yes, perhaps. That's what I thought. It needs to be considered.'

`It takes a lot of work to research a single family. To do five would be onerous.' But there was more than this bothering me, though, in an abstract way, I'd also been thinking of those names . `What do you think it might prove?'

`I don't know. Basic research often has no immediate application, you know. But it may provide you with knowledge useful elsewhere.'

I thought about it a moment, and knew then I would not be able to do it. There were beginning to be other things I needed to write about. `I haven't the time, David.'

`No. But I have. And it is history, after all. I shall enjoy it.'

We rattled the cutlery and crockery around, clearing up a Saturday morning breakfast as the best of couples do it. David had disappeared, ostensibly to get the weekend paper, and, the television silent, Penny was either with him or ensconced with her own reading matter in some corner of the house. I sensed some mice of mine very close to coming out of the woodwork.

Tarrasco, perhaps. After all, they were both representatives of the law, but it was somehow hard to see this woman as no different from a man on a mission, hellbent as he had been. And hellbent as I would have been, with him.

`Cameron five, Alastair three.'

Angie looked at me as if I were juggling some of David's best glasses.

`I'm afraid it's a little like the Lions and the Christians.' But I was still deliberately obfuscating, so I took the breath necessary. `I brought death to three, just as Cameron felt he had to five.'

She put the cloth down, making some sort of automatic drying motion on the countertop. Then she took a step closer, really the only step left to take. `I know. I called Toronto and talked to someone called Jack. He said you needed help.'

It washed over me, that tide of despair, and I cried as Penny never could. But Angie's arms were warm, and her breast gave me solace, enough, at least, to feel that utter exhaustion of release, the catharsis necessary if life is ever going to get better.

Penny found me like that.

David didn't, but as I had Penny in my arms when he came whistling up the hallway, slapping the paper against the wall as if giving all the spirits in hell notice that he was coming, he read her mood, and nodded. `Good man.' Then, as if it were the weather that was in his mind. `Don't get many days better than this.'

The morning *was* one of those rare fall days when everybody says `Indian summer', but it was no time to be obtuse. He, after all, was part of the gift. `Penny and I thought we'd go and get a bottle,' I said.

`I want bubbles in it,' said Penny.

Honour. I thought, no, knew that was it. Cameron had sacrificed his life for it; I had run. Had I been Peruvian, there would have been some sort of accounting even had I not done the killing. But my friendship with Carlos brought privilege, an exemption from due process that had let me refuse Tarrasco's plan with impunity. I'd turned my back on it all. Walked away.

Had Grandmother been alive I think she would have been disappointed. Perhaps she had held her only grandson in too much esteem, giving him all her time when he was able to make some for her. Had it inflated my head, led me to think myself more than I was? But Cameron put a face on honour, took it as his comfort, his ultimate solace, to his early, dishonoured grave. In comparison I had mocked all standards of decency and refused to put any effort into apprehending killers to whom I had given three lives.

Grandmother's hand. The thought formed.

Fred Webster ran rough, black-nailed fingers across the drawings. `Nothing like I ever knew him to work on. These aren't engineering drawings. Closer to fluid mechanics really, but far too regular a structure to be close to real world processes. You'd never find just a couple of inlet pipes leading to so many outlets; see, the valves point in that direction, so flow is from few to many. Pressure would be dropping all along the way.'

I'd come to Fred because I thought that he, of all the staff at the Department, might be able to answer my questions. `What about the labels?'

`Seem almost to be straightforward binary code, except for the dashes and commas. May have been the old man's shorthand system. Hey, sorry Alastair; no disrespect meant.' He looked genuinely crestfallen. `I liked him a lot. I'm one of the few around here that actually knew him.' He looked more closely. ''Course, the labels might mean diameter changes; if they were pipes, I mean. But it's not the normal way to signify diameter.'

'Do you remember him being secretive?'

'Not really. He didn't need to be. He was streets ahead of any of us in practical engineering terms, so we tended to catch up with him on the theory once his stuff was in place.'

Fred's office spoke to a similar though less original practicality, stark, with a few blueprints tacked to the walls. A photo on the desk showed him with a woman of similar age and some small children, whom I thought were probably grandchildren. There was none of the litter of the modern theoretical mind, which tends to prefer disorder in the office environment.

'So you don't really know what these are.'

'The old man was in a field that today we would split up into robotics and controls. Manipulator designs and positioning systems. This is nothing to do with that. Sorry. But leave one with me. No, a copy would be better. I'll take a crack at the binary code. See if the standard table works.' He saw me looking puzzled. 'All numbers can be represented by zeros and ones. It's the combination of those two digits that tells you what number they represent. Anyone used to doing it could write this code from his head if all he wanted was to represent something alphanumerically. I'm a bit rusty, so I'll have to work it out longhand. Give me a day or so.' He took one of the drawings out into the hall, and there was the almost instant whir and snap of a photocopier. Someone must have come up to him, because he said 'Trying to solve a puzzle for Alastair MacNeil. One of the old man's drawings, see?' But he came back to the office alone, and no-one followed nor passed by the door. 'There you go,' and he handed the original back.

Walking that hallway was to take up the gauntlet, because it was almost certain that I'd run into her. I'd left her a note saying where I was, but if she'd heard about the fire, and wondered about my well-being, she had not phoned to find out.

Her office was three doors down from Fred's, though the door had been closed when I'd arrived so I had no way of knowing whether she was inside. But as I left Fred's office, I saw immediately that the door was open. I thought of turning to go in the opposite direction, but knew that I had to make my own amends. Then she came to the door.

'Hello, Alastair.'

'Nancy.'

'Come in.' She made to turn back as she spoke, but something may have told her that I might not obey so she checked her movement and watched me as I walked slowly towards her. She only moved in as I reached her doorway. 'Visiting Fred, were you?' I understood that it had been Nancy to whom Fred had made that comment while photocopying.

'Yes.'

The hall stayed strangely empty, no faces peering around doorframes at the quarrel.

Honour is the price with which respect is bought. But if honour slips, not only silver tarnishes. It is more complicated if that price is self-assessed, for one has no means of objective valuation; then it is a matter of conscience and one's own understanding of moral obligation. Some have no conscience at all, though this is relative to the dictates of the begetting culture; others, likewise, take conscience to extreme.

Cameron's case was one of contrast: the court saw it necessary to exact the ultimate price, though with no intent to restore any honour to the condemned; Cameron, considering himself innocent, required that price of himself in order to die with dignity.

Quandary is a word of uncertain origin - it sprang into language for reasons subsequently forgotten. Had I considered myself blameless of the mayhem around me in Peru I should have seen no quandary, but equally I would be conscienceless in a society that stills holds honour important somewhere on its fringes. But I was in fact carrying a terrible guilt, so my quandary was how to assess my own price so that I should, at some point in the future, be able to live in peace. I was coming to know what it was, but not how to pay it.

Later that week I sat down with David. 'Anderson and Greaves appear to go nowhere,' he said. 'Lattimore and Horrocks are a little better. But it's Whittaker you should take a look at. Family is still around. D'you want to see?'

He spread one of several sheets of paper across the table, an aggregation of smaller sheets held together by transparent tape. He had a neat, small hand, and I had to look closely to see what was written as the main title. His sleuthing had taken hold of him and the previous afternoon he'd disappeared to use the genealogical records at the public library.

The lines fanned horizontally, from a box on the far left, to a stack of boxes on the far right. Names, and dates of birth and death filled the boxes, and marriage dates were written in over the lines. Phillip Whittaker, said the title. Seven generations had given rise to more than a hundred people, Whittaker himself having married Edna Levan and done his best to populate Upper Canada. But child death rates had been high, and many lines ended in earlier boxes, somewhere in the middle of the page.

`Main line is still that of farmers. These three, here, here and there, today own almost contiguous parcels of land. It was so easy, that I managed to find some of them through the phone book. Actually went this morning and talked to old Mrs Catterick, Alma Whittaker that was. That's her there. She pulled out a bible that had come down in her line and filled a lot of it in for me. Had to drink a lot of tea. But she knew nothing about 1814 herself, and called me back after lunch to say none of the other core members of the family did either.'

It was almost inevitable that if any of Cameron's five compatriots had gone back to farming there would still be sign around, for Loyalist country is proud of its century heritage, farms that are still in the family one hundred years from the date of Confederation. Though Confederation was half a century later than Cameron's death, and so not a birth itself that necessarily carried significance. But it was the idea that mattered. Young countries look for signals that indicate stability and prosperity; Loyalist families were no different. And the country had been prosperous to a degree, even if longevity on the land also owed itself to frugality. Century farmers remember their roots, and Alma Catterick (née Whittaker) generally remembered hers. Her grandchildren were among the rightmost column. I ran down the surnames, somehow expecting one to jump out at me, but they were all as ordinary as Whittaker, and all as unknown.

`No,' said David. `Nothing there, right? Too easy.' But even if it hadn't been easy, I wasn't sure what we'd be looking for. Or whom. `This is Lattimore. And this,' pulling over another sheet, `is Horrocks. Not much to go on yet.' In each case a couple of lines meandered across the page, but none got to the present. `If I can complete these two, you'll have three out of five. Sixty percent probability of providing you with the right information, if genealogy were to get you there in the first place.' Again it sounded a bit like a lecture: an historian using science to value his information. But he was enjoying it, and perhaps he'd find a name that rang a bell, or someone else who had arcane knowledge to share.

`Thanks for the effort.'

`Oh no. It's no effort at all.'

Angela came home just as I was leaving. A charcoal gray suit offset the brighter blouse below it, saying that this was a serious woman. Low square heels tapped the hall floor, and lips brushed my cheek as I took her hand. 'Not staying for dinner?'

'I must go out. Something unfinished from yesterday.'

'Will we see you later?'

'Perhaps around ten if you're still up?'

'I'd like that.'

'Mm. OK'

I left the University library about 9.30pm. The fact that I was going home to Angela was a consequence of fate, not a decision consciously taken. Nevertheless, I felt easier about it, and, if I were honest, happy.

'Business taken care of?' She had changed, and was sitting in one of the chairs listening to some music. A fire was burning in the grate.

I nodded. 'Summer music for a winter's night?'

She smiled. 'I think back sometimes. I like summer.'

As I poured the wine I was conscious of why I had recently refused it. This brought Angela into sharp focus, and I looked at her in a way that I hadn't with Nancy. Her sexuality was quite different, more rounded, perhaps, though this had nothing to do with a fuller figure. I think she was quite aware of me doing it, though I hoped she was not able to read my mind. She shifted slightly, and I heard the whisper of fabric moving. I looked into my glass and reproved myself for my thoughts.

'I've decided to go back to Peru.'

She showed no surprise. 'I think that has been coming ever since I've known you.'

'Guilt-laden, you mean?'

'Not at all. More a battle with decency, and wondering how to do it.'

'I didn't think I'd really given it much thought.'

She shook her head. 'Every moment of your analysis of Cameron has been your own introspective search.'

`I am him and he is me.'

`Apart from the historical context, completely.'

`Grandmother's hand. Showing me the way.'

`It's too simple to think that, beyond death, she knew what to give you. She left you something before death that would have fitted almost any stage of your life. Something you would need.'

I looked into the fire, the warmth fitting the last notes of summer music, and saw Grandmother in those sunnier times. A sense of her came and went in an instant.

`When will you go?' asked Angela.

I thought a moment. `As soon as I can. While I still have the courage.'

`It's nothing to do with courage. It's what you want to do.'

`It's what I have to do.'

`Not in the first instance - the wanting is more important. I'd rather think of you doing it for that.'

`Will you think of me while I'm doing it?'

`You've come into our house, now - haven't you understood that? None of us will forget you.'

`Thank you. But I don't really think that is what I was asking.'

She laughed. `I didn't, either. But you've got to get something out of your system first, haven't you?'

I had absolutely no idea if she was talking about Peru, or the price she might have thought Cameron's existence demanded.

God

L *avo mis manos de tí,* Alastair.' I wash my hands of you. Carlos was stricken beyond belief when I said what it was I intended to do. He didn't mean it or say it unkindly, but neither could I go into Tarrasco's plan, the *Mayor* and I agreeing that nobody should know of our intent, and only those Andean telegraphs which had sounded before, sounding now. And I wanted absolutely nothing to happen which could come back and haunt Carlos, at some time in the future.

But in my attempt to repay my own debt, to him and to the others, there was the very real possibility that I would cause my own death. Where, between acknowledging that, as a debt, this would be only right, and the other extreme of fighting all with a very fierce will to live, should I draw the line? Part of that same quandary: how could I go back and face that same village, knowing that I would, in all probability, bring down that same blight once again. Tarrasco said it in a different way: 'How can we think of using somewhere else? You are associated with that place, now and forever. Go back and dig.' But it made it no easier, even if the people now had even more practice in suffering, because there was no guarantee that further death could be avoided.

I had had to deal with different sorts of signals, one of which had been beaten into me. And if I were to do what Tarrasco wanted, which required that I retrace certain paths, it was with both fear and scorn that I went back to that other dark sanctuary, repeating that visit which courtesy required. The scorn was simple: that *Generalísimo* Pablo López Martín was even less of a protector of the people than for which I had originally given him possible credit. The fear was that the man, as the uniformed deity of the region (his rank, only, deifying the uniform), would disallow any rural travel. My best hope was that he would, again, disavow responsibility for my safety. Tarrasco had said I was far safer in *his* hands.

López had not sent anyone to see me after I'd been brought off the *puna*, but a possible lapse in procedure did not seem to be on his mind. 'You did not heed my advice, *señor*

MacNeil. Instead, I believe you learned a hard lesson.' He was distant, and intimidating.

`I was present at three murders, *General*. The lessons were several.'

That rancid look came back. `You wish to play games with words?'

`I merely suggested that there was more than one lesson, *General*, and that they could be learnt by others as well as by me.'

`Implying?' It was the demand of a superior to a new ranker, the tone glacial.

But then I had to be cautious, for Tarrasco had said that if I pushed him too far, anger would replace reason and I'd just be kicked right out of his Department. I had to push him no further than to make him see the importance of acceding to my request. `That providing security to such a large and mountainous region is extremely difficult, and that all are in danger. It is impossible for your men to be everywhere, all of the time.'

It had caught him short, and he was still for a moment. Then, some sort of reason re-established: `You are quite right. My men do what they can, of course, but we are at the mercy of Lima. We cannot patrol everywhere.'

`You were good enough to give me your blessing before, *General*.' An easy lie. `You will not object if I go back? I will assume my own risk.'

He had stared at me. `You wish to go back? *Por Dios!* I should have thought you had come close enough to death to wish never to see the *puna* again. You learned no lesson at all.'

I was, frankly, tired of lessons. `Not quite, *General*. I have a debt to repay to those who died. I should like to do it my way.' Or Tarrasco's, really. But I was central to the whole thing.

`We have little time here for people who wish to do things their way, *señor* MacNeil.' But he had been thinking while he spoke. `Go, then. But do not come running back to me with another tale of failure.'

It is almost impossible for sweat to run at just under four thousand metres, because it dries almost before it leaves the pores. But, as that door closed behind me, I had felt it trickle down my spine, signal of a further lesson in fear.

The faces were silent, hostile, when they saw me approaching the village. Tarrasco's man played no part in explaining my return beyond his role as a guide. I asked to see the village leader, aware that a lot hinged on his willingness to see me. Refusal had to be carefully avoided.

`*Sientese, señor.*` Sit down. The walls had been chinked with brown mud, holding in the high-altitude, rank body odour of people that found it unnecessary to wash very often. The earth floor had been swept, the brushmarks a fish-scale pattern in different tones. Rough wooden benches lined the walls, and I had sat where indicated, the bench rocking slightly under me. My guide stayed outside.

`Permit me, first, to thank you for whatever help you gave me in taking me down.` These were gracious people, even if grindingly poor, so it had been necessary to find equivalent language. Down, meant off the *puna*.

`The *señor* was badly hurt. For him to live required more care than we thought we could give. His medicine is different from ours.`

And so it had been, that night, when I, alone, was left alive. `It was necessary for me to come back to thank you. And to express my deepest apologies for my contribution to that tragedy.`

`We all die, *señor*, and God will take some of us by tortuous paths. It happened because He wished it.`

It was too easy to dismiss simplicity in Faith as something facile; I had no doubt that he believed what he said. But he was also being polite, not wanting to concur with any catalytic role of mine, nor, particularly, wanting my apology. `Had I not been present, perhaps the others would still be alive.`

`That is just what I mean. He wished it then, because the *señor* was there.` He sat in stolid acceptance of higher-order management, earth-crusted toes splaying out of the ends of his sandals, and a hat of no discernably different colour holding his eyes steady under its brim. His associates in the village hierarchy sat on either side, some looking at me, some with their thoughts much further away. None was happy to have me present, now. But the message was quite clear: I *had* been to blame.

`Would you permit me to stay among you, now? To give you help in whatever you would have me do?` Go and dig, Tarrasco had said. So if they put me to work conserving what little soil they had left to farm, I'd meet his command to the letter.

It caused some surprise, and it was hard to determine whether they found the initial idea agreeable. There was an interchange in *quechua*, and one or two of the elders got up and left, perhaps in disagreement. But it became clear that they were willing to listen to me, that nobody had yet persuaded them to a consensus on kicking me out. `Our life is perhaps harder than the *señor* could imagine. Poor food, no comfort.` He hadn't mentioned the water, which there was very little of, and which would almost certainly be filthy.

But one had to be careful with their pride, because that hard life engendered it. 'For that reason I should like you to have me.' A cynic might have said it built character. But there had been no place for cynicism nor condescension here; I had to show that I was open to anything they wanted.

One of the two elders came back, leading a sad-looking woman. *Quechua* flowed again, and the woman made a negative motion, avoiding looking at me. The village leader said something else, and her eyes finally passed over me, and she made a slight shrug. He turned to me, also taking his time looking for words. 'Maria is unhappy with the thought of your sharing her house. But we have explained that she is to show you no favour. If you stay with her, you will agree to helping her in the fields she owns.'

So I thought her most probably a widow, for no husband had been consulted in the process, though women controlled and worked the land as much as the men. 'Thank you.'

'Dolores was her sister. She, with her husband, died that night.'

Dolores; a good Catholic Christian name. *Dolor*, in Spanish, means pain, something that we Anglicans, so much further from the linguistic roots of some of our names, forget when we name our daughters. So Maria was probably her unmarried sister, and had lost all her partners in work when that tragedy brought the most painful extinction imaginable. I said nothing, any verbal expression of sorrow impossibly trite when one has condemned a middle-aged woman to a solitary life of backbreaking manual labour. I just got up and followed her out of the door.

The soil was dreadfully thin, and in many places more than half stone. The small plot of land was in the midst of many others, small stone walls separating some, but the rest open and what little vegetation on it grazed right to the ground. Ragged sheep pottered around, looking for anything left to nibble, herded by ragged youngsters even smaller than the animals themselves. Both animals and children were very dirty.

'*Chakitaklia*,' she said, pointing at something she'd put in my hand. It wasn't much more than a long stick with a small platform lashed just above and behind the steel chisel head. She made thrusting and stepping motions, and for one idiotic moment I thought I was supposed to break into a dance. Then she grabbed it from me, and showed me how, perhaps for millennia, High Andean peoples had cultivated the soil. By chakitaklia. Lesson over, she gave it back and walked away.

It took me half an hour to find my own rhythm, hampered by muscles unused to hard labour, and lungs unused to providing the necessary oxygen at four thousand metres. I had to take frequent breaks to keep ragged breathing at an acceptable level. Slowly my patch of cultivated soil grew in size, though a rapid calculation suggested that the whole plot, at my rate of work, would take me several days. That second lesson humbled me more than the first.

'We will have to move slowly and carefully,' Tarrasco had said. 'By the time you get there, I will have my men nearby, but I cannot keep them together in a single troop or the word will spread very quickly. You will be close to a trade route, so let us say just that there will be more *llamas* than usual moving to and fro. Another reason why you should return there.'

But I had still been unsure. 'Can you be close enough to be there in time?'

'I think so, yes. But it will depend on when and where we catch their movement.'

'And if you miss them completely?' It had been easy to sweat just thinking about it, and I had become more than a little damp.

'Do not forget our other means. We will monitor both radio and movement. If anyone goes anywhere or says anything, we will know.'

But it had all sounded inadequate, and now that I was here it left me no easier. I was surrounded by massive spaces, stretching across distant hills to snow-covered peaks. Small figures worked other plots, the freshly-worked earth sharp stains on the grazed-smooth soil. How I had thought Tarrasco could provide me with any protection at all withered under sudden, crushing agoraphobia, and I howled a maniacal laugh to the sky. Oh Jesus bloody Christ.

The punishment eased only after a few hours. I saw community members slowly coming in from their fields, gathering around a slow fire that had burned all morning. A small boy came to get me. '*A comer, señor,*' making mouth-stuffing movements. I leaned my chakitaklia against a rock and followed him, hunger a pain in my belly. Other hands no cleaner than the dirt they worked scrabbled under the ashes on the fringes of the fire, pulled out blackened, oval objects, and passed them to me. They peeled into the steaming golden-yellow flesh of baked potatoes. Nothing had ever tasted better.

But perhaps that golden moment in time, when hunger was abated and satisfaction took on the simplest dimension possible, was meant to be, and to be remembered. For none followed. Surprise works best when it is least expected, and I had not even considered an immediate, disastrous end. Even in my high anxiety, I'd allowed Tarrasco his right to be sure he could deal with evil, and at a price that would be more than reasonable. I, at least, forgot that evil always demands the highest price possible.

I was aware of no more than a sudden movement among the others, something behind me catching their attention, and the echoed beginnings of a frantic shout. Echoed, because something else turned everything black, and only sound stayed with me in that falling cage that took me straight to the underworld, and night.

It becomes less hard, as each day passes, to understand the end. Oh, understand is perhaps not the right word, because this is no smart man's debate, just the vision of my own step into the next world. But I know not enough of this one to want to leave it yet, and how can one leave love without the greatest pain imaginable? The hanging's pain will be small, compared.

It were a clever plan, and I fell for it, and because I fell, I must pay. The cost was to the others, because they, Duncan, Honor and the men, were charged with instant silence, though I doubt they can have gone quietly. And, in my moments alone, here in this cell, when the mice run across the boards, and my stump of a candle has finally burnt itself to the table, no more light till the morrow, well, then, I weep for them.

It were not Chauncey, directly, that put me here. But that is all I will say.

It was no more than a fog, at first, and bitter cold. If it were not night, then something else kept the light from my eyes, though the pain in my head was such that I might already be completely blind, the fog the only relief. But it was a fog that roiled through thought and sense as well, because I could not remember who I was, nor what I was.

Sound, though, began to take on some structure, away from a bleating waveform, slowly taking the form of voice. The brain showed itself further sensate by telling me that this was a language I understood, and that if only *I* listened I would understand. But I hurt too much to want to comply, so I went back into that fog, and let everything rest a while.

In the end, some deep-seated will to bring the disparate elements of the body back together, brought touch, sound and taste into the foreground, letting me know I was trussed to something rough, that there *was* the occasional word being spoken that I could understand, and that I had blood in my mouth. But a rag across my eyes kept light out of them, and there was no smell at all. That same returning consciousness told me this last was odd. More than just the cold made me shiver, and the body curled in an attempt to vomit.

`Se despertó.` He's awake.

`Leave him. Let him think about it a while.`

Think. Nothing that I seemed very capable of, though the mind was pressing on me to remember where I got the headache from. Then the reaction from the nausea kicked in, and acid scorched the walls of my belly. But that made me want to vomit again. So I vowed to myself not to think about potatoes. Potatoes. Oh Jesus bloody Christ. I vomited for real, knowing both the cause of the pain and the evil.

`You hit him too hard.`

`Lo siento, capitán.` I'm sorry. Capitán.

But there is nothing in mine own book that says I shall not write what I feel, for if I write it not, then how, Alice, Father, Mother, will you understand what I take with me? No, not what they say I take, but that which I say I take. I should have the right to define the difference.

For understand that throughout this war we have been beset by hypocrisy and scorn; as much as it comes from Washington, so could it come from Whitehall. No! Stay with me; do not cast me aside on such a flimsy hearing. For I think the truth lies in greed, so in greed should you seek it, if ever you are to accept my current circumstance. Remember, if that extravagant democracy against which we fight, fights for the cause of commerce and gain, then it would not be strange to find similar greed at the bottom of this? So, do not think that all wish for the same, satisfactory, end.

And I do feel, believe me, all of you, but thee in particular, Alice. For, cast in this role that was not of my choosing, there is anger at what I know will stick to our name. There is also anger that I should have to carry a burden of honour so heavy that I have but the one recourse, and that is to present myself before the others so that they may see my sorrow with it. And, if God wills it and they do to, that I may be forgiven.

So the telegraph had sent its signal, an Andean semaphore pinpointing me for the taking. Carlos had been right, completely crazy. But only the blood in my mouth was bitter, for the knowledge that I had set myself up for this would allow no other reaction than a cold sense of death. Nor had I any right to bitterness beyond pure hate for whoever killed innocent people, and for he who was instrumental in my massively pounding headache. I vomited again.

`Si vomites más, te mataré.` If you puke again I'll kill you.

`Fuck off.`

`Que?! What did you say?`

`Give me some water.`

I heard him get up, but he crossed the floor away from me. `You'll get water when I want to give it to you. Perhaps just before you die. Hit him again, but leave the head alone.` And the instruction given, he went out.

The literal sense of the command was ignored, and the pain slowly transferred itself elsewhere, intensifying as both stick and foot explored ribs and thighs. Disobedience, I thought, losing count of the blows, sure he'd been told only to hit me once, is a major cause of failure. But it was not carefully thought, as I was slowly losing what tenuous consciousness I had to a red haze, a fire behind my blindfold. Dolores, you should see me now.

If I think about this carefully, I find it difficult to recall from whence came that first whisper. Oh, I knew that the words were from Jeremiah, and now I know that he paid the price, both for the knowing, and for the telling. But it were more than passing strange, for, of all of us on that side of the water, it were Jeremiah who understood both risk and caution, the latter his byword. So, someone knew, and someone else was told.

But, Chauncey was required to risk cannon that I know he would not want open to any threat. And the probability that he would lose them doubled when Spilsbury - commanding the Royal George, and, with fair wind, posted at the harbour mouth - also heard of the convoy, and led a fleet of smaller boats to where he fell in with Popham. Spilsbury's was separate intelligence, but he was taken with Popham, and, as Popham's blame is mine, Spilbury's is mine also.

So I calculate that Chauncey chanced the wind, thinking it to stay in his favour longer, and that his agent caused that first whisper, somewhere close to Jeremiah's ear. And that, and our movements subsequently planned, were the end of it all.

Time passes, and the body lies like a log on the dirt, not quite insensate, for it knows that it lies there, victim of its own folly. The head throbs from the first, earlier, blow, but the ribs ache from the later ones, and ache to the point where the smallest expansion of the rib cage, to draw in that low-density Andean air, is agony. But the body must do it, not only because there is that metabolical demand for oxygen, but also because it feels anger, and, by clinging to life, it knows that it may have a chance, a ridiculously slim chance, to get even.

Fuck it, Dolores, I hate these bastards.

Sleep barely comes, for which I am thankful: it is a luxury I do not wish, cannot afford. I know, without confirmation from the Court, that I will hang. So in my time left I think of thee, Alice, our son Duncan, Mother and Father, and all our friends. I think of the five who should not have died in the ways they did. And I think of why they died, how they did. And I find that darkness is the best time to find answers, perhaps because God is with me momentarily at such time, wishing me to understand the root of my punishment. But I am sore pressed to see with His clarity, and can only do so with mine. Which is, apart from the flashes of light He brings, as dim as this cell with no taper. But one may, without mathematick, add things up, which I have done.

Where is that sod Tarrasco?

Had I not stayed with Carlos on various occasions, I should not have understood the dawn's polyphony - Bach's St Mathew's Passion, sung by a castrati choir, which, stumbling through the parts not yet learned, hummed it instead. So, only that told me it was dawn, as my blindfold was completely lightproof, and my guard was still snoring somewhere close to me.

But that beautiful sound told me that there was a herd of alpaca penned somewhere quite close, wanting to be let out to the grazing ground, and that those same animals had spotted some sort of movement. My brain sorted this information more rapidly than the day before, suggesting general recovery from the blow to the head. Hunger suggested that the rest of me was in improving condition, though bonds and aching bruises belied any chances of immediate and rapid movement. I was as captive as the alpaca, though considerably less interested in humming anything. Instead, I was angry, and wanting to take that anger out on whoever gave me the chance to do so. I saw no likelihood that the day would bring the opportunity.

Only my hands were loosened when they brought a bowl of gruel and some cold potatoes. The guard shuffled around the hut, different noises the indication of his body accommodating to the new day. Once I'd eaten he hauled me to my feet and led me outside. ` Cinco minutos,` he said. Five minutes, to complete my own bodily functions. ` No toques el trapo.` Don't touch the blindfold. He shuffled away, but as far as I knew the whole valley had come and was standing around watching me.

` Eres periodista.` You're a journalist. It was my captor, back from wherever he'd spent the night, arriving on foot and only briefly checking with the guard on the details of my behaviour. He did not ask me, however, so his concern was not for my comfort.

I had not told him this, either before or now. ` Why do you think that?'

` What does that matter? I ask the questions.' The voice was low, as if he wished no-one else to hear.

There seemed no point in answering so I shrugged.

` Why did you come back? What is there here to write about? Who are you writing it for?' But his speech was not that of his subordinates. Andean, certainly, but urban, the way a schoolteacher or a minor public official might talk. As I couldn't see him, the characteristics of his diction seemed the only thing that gave him character. Apart from his hate.

` I came back because I owed something to these people.'

` You owed something? To these peasants? You're out of your mind.'

This seemed a familiar reaction. ` Perhaps.'

` Why does a rich extranjero like yourself think he owes anything to a poor Andean campesino?'

` Why do you assume that because I'm a foreigner I'm rich?'

` My friend, all you foreigners have more money than brains. It is both those faults that bring you here. To meddle in business not your own. You think you have the secret to a better life, that you have something these people would wish to have if only they understood you. You think you can empower them so that they may throw off their oppressive yoke. Isn't that right?'

` If you say so.' I had no intention of this being more than a one-sided dialectic.

'Have you ever thought that they want nothing else? That they live quite happily if no-one suggests that there is a better life if only they do this or that?'

'I thought that was precisely what people like *you* did, when they come out of the night to kill.'

'You think I'm a killer?'

'I know so, remember?'

'Pity for you. It makes any alternative so much harder.'

He came and went several times that day. Each time he would start with the same questions: *What is there here to write about? Who are you writing for?* Each time I gave him answers he didn't like: *I came back because I wanted to. I write for myself. Poverty is instructive.* Each time I was kicked for my trouble. I grew to recognize his step, understanding how the blind develop compensatory senses. But his voice changed not a whit. Low, deadly, with a bored patience that said answers were irrelevant.

'You think you are God.' This time I gave him no time to ask his own questions.

'I am to you. You'd better understand that. I hold you in my hand.'

'Only because someone else gives you that power.'

'What do you mean, someone else?'

'You are waiting for something. Perhaps someone. This means that you are dependent on others. That they are in control, not you. You would have killed me by now if you were acting on your own - I would be too much of a risk, otherwise.'

'I am as I said, so take care or I will kill you as I wish.'

'You may be my gaoler, but you will wait for an order to do that.'

'I wait for no orders. If you try my patience any more you will find that out.' This time, both the voice and the beating were harder.

If I am ever able to write about this, I thought, I shall be no less God than you.

There was no sight nor sound of Tarrasco. I thought it and laughed at myself. I couldn't see, because of the blindfold, and I had no idea what he'd sound like. No bugle-blaring cavalry to the rescue, anyway. It would have to be a sudden surprise, perhaps following the soft-padded footfalls of his llama train. But there was not even that. Just the return of the alpaca herd, led by someone familiar to both my guard and my gaoler. The choir was silent, and so was the night.

Another day passed and I spent most of it shitting. By the time evening came I had voided several times what I had consumed, and was dizzy from the dehydration. The irony was that it was probably the water that they gave me to drink which made me sick in the first place. Dozing gave the only relief. When I stumbled outside, hands on a short cord tied to my foot hobble, I cared not whether the whole world watched. My guard didn't venture beyond the door: ` *Cuente sus pasos,*' count your steps, `and make sure it's half a step less each time.' He turned back in laughing.

Dozing took me into the nether regions of my mind, just short of full sleep, where the images were strong and actions vibrant. The crossing into Cameron's world was seamless, as it had been two days before when they first beat me unconscious and I had been unable to distinguish between the then and the now. *I am you and you are me.* I sat through those final hours in the cell, understanding why I was there, and heard the rattle of keys which heralded my last few minutes on earth. Maighster Craig stood behind the figure of the gaoler, bible in hand. I passed him my scribblings, for such they seemed, and asked for nothing more than a short prayer. The way to the scaffold seemed lit by something beyond light, and I needed no guidance to find it. The hood placed on my head served no purpose at all as I could see right through it, and there were Alice, Mother, Father, and, yes, Duncan and Honor and the others all to see me take that last long step. And suddenly there was weightlessness. But before the rope reached its limit there was a stabbing pain in my belly, and I awoke once more to go outside and shit.

`Why do they call you *capitán?*'

He had come and gone just as the day before, but had perhaps decided that there was little point anymore in beating me. I'd given him no answers to his questions, and had become fully convinced that we were waiting for something else to happen. What, I had no idea.

But it was a stupid question because it was personal, and people such as him do not like their captives crossing over onto private ground. So it brought a beating, but just as I passed out from a kick that, unlike the others, missed my ribs and smacked into the tender spot on the side of my head, he said: `*Porque fui.*' Because I was.

146

'You'd better have no shit left inside you. There won't be time to stop.'

There was more movement around me than there had been at any time in the last two days, and at least another set of footfalls that was new. I was hauled to my feet and led out of the hut. The foot hobble was removed, and my hands retied behind my back. Earlier I had heard the alpaca return, but they were still silent so I thought it about midnight. As we left I felt the eyes of that solitary shepherd, staying behind with his animals, watch my stumbling figure following behind three men, and I wondered whether he thought at all about where they were taking me and what would happen there.

After a day in my new abode, still hobbled, I saw that there were two views open to me. One was the dirty stone wall of the hut, its small walled surrounding fields and the endless Andean sky. The other was his face, across which little flitted. The former, outside at least, was picturesque. But it was nothing to my future, apart from being a landscape across which I (fervently) hoped help would come. Like the watched pot, however, I thought it probably a landscape which would refuse to boil.

Somehow I knew that that face and the mind behind it were the landscape I should focus on. Even as dirty as the hut, I was sure the face too had stone walls surrounding the interior fields of the mind, most perhaps as weedy and barren as the small plots outside, but perhaps one or two where the most valuable thoughts were kept. One, I knew, was nothing more than a midden. How to start a conversation?

'D'you know Tarrasco, the policeman?'

His eyes flickered over to me, then went back to that point in inner space where his vision had been focussed.

I pushed. 'An interesting man. Creative.'

He held his breath a moment, then let it out in a sigh. 'You think he can help you?'

'I wasn't thinking about that. I was making a comparison.'

He frowned a little. 'You were comparing him to me? What would make you do that?'

'So you do know him.'

He took a moment to answer. 'Not necessarily.'

I barked a sort of nervous laugh. 'Necessarily? What an odd word.'

His smile was a mask over the fixed features of his skull. 'I know of many policemen. I should not necessarily know of the one you mention.'

I knew, or had known a few moments before, that it was a lie, that he did know Tarrasco.

Or knew of him. Given Tarrasco's zonal authority, it was unlikely that many people would not know of him. 'Is he one to fear?'

Should I fear any, perhaps I would him. Perhaps he thought it, perhaps he didn't. It was obvious that something was moving among those stone walls, but he wasn't about to show me what. He got up from his post against the wall, swung open the rough wooden door and went out. The odour of stale sweat stayed. The door sat open on its leather hinges, foot in the dust, and I saw a vulture on the wing. Not a good sight.

At some point in the day, more potatoes and a viscous, bitter coffee. I was left alone to eat, and consumed both with an avid hunger, grateful for how they each met needs I had not before recognized as distinct. But not an expeditionary force with extensive supply lines, I thought. Apart from the coffee I suspected that they were unearthing the tubers from the surrounding plots as they were needed.

The door had stayed open after that earlier departure. I saw that the light was changing, and suddenly had a different need. 'Can I come out to watch the sunset?' I called.

My captor's shadow darkened the portal, and he leant against the jamb. He had his knife in hand, and was cleaning the ashes and potato skin from under his fingernails. 'You think it may be your last?'

'Even if it were the next-to-last I'd like to see it.'

He stropped the knife-blade against his leg, then turned to peruse the small yard in front of the hut. Having apparently considered his options he pointed with the knife to a nook in the low stone wall. 'There. Sit on the ground and watch your sun. If I say move, crawl back into the hut without a word.' He went out.

It took me some time to stand, because I'd lain prone for several hours and both my knees and back were stiff. The hobble allowed only mincing steps, so I took each one carefully, working the muscles in each leg as I did so. They turned warm as the blood flowed again. Then the heat of the sun embraced my back as I left the shade of the house. I sat where instructed.

The view from inside the hut had shown me little but the surrounding walled fields. From my new seat, however, I had several ranges of mountains in front of me, each more distant one reaching higher until the furthest succeeded in cloaking itself in snow. I closed my eyes and soared above, seeing the hut and its fields as no more than a small blemish against an eternal geography. Somehow the trance lasted, until another thought brought me back to earth and I recognized that I truly was far from anywhere safe.

The sun went down.

He slept badly. Perhaps he did not trust the watch, and felt that only he would know if danger threatened. Or perhaps he sensed as many unknowns as I did, and sorting through each of them kept the subconscious continually active, and spilling energy over into the dreaming mind. Not that he talked in his sleep, but he was not a man at rest.

Neither was I. I was cold and sore. The ground seemed to press hard against my shoulder and pelvis if I laid on my side, and my head and buttocks if I laid on my back. But it seemed logical to me that the gravitational pull of the planet should be that much greater when then was an extra three thousand metres of rock beneath my earthen bed, so I convinced myself that my comfort was not going to increase, and drowsed.

But each movement of his brought me instantly awake. At intervals he would rise and approach the door. He would listen intently, then make a small noise. A similar sound would come from outside, reassuring him, and he would return to his slumbers. Each time I grew to listen for it, as he did. Each time I felt it better that we should both hear it than that we should both hear nothing. Each time I felt more inclined to ask him what he would do if the responding noise did not come. But my fear of one of the possible answers kept me quiet.

Dawn came without that final test.

I think they had removed the blindfold earlier because it could be an impediment to rapid movement, the starlit Andean night showing almost everything in some sort of vast chiaroscuro, and motion visible at some distance. One of the three men constantly worked as vanguard, whistling signals back to my captor. Once the latter knocked me to the ground at the sound of an urgent trill, but we were soon back to a rapid trot across the *puna*. I saw no villages, and had no idea whether we avoided any. One or two constellations that I recognized from high Canadian skies dragged their way across the horizon.

I became an encumbrance after a while, still weak from the diarrhoea, and hungry from the earlier lack of appetite. I began to fall frequently, tripping on clumps of low vegetation, or unbalanced by small potholes. The patience of my companion wore thinner, and he began to hit me across the back with a short stick each time I fell. I could have told him that such actions were counterproductive, for the pain was a distraction to the control of my feet, but such a comment seemed to me against my own interests because I might then get to where I was going faster. It had occurred to me much earlier that that specific destination might not be one to enjoy. I had also thought that becoming a nuisance might also result in distraction and rescue, though I'd lost faith in Tarrasco and gave that outcome little probability. But the anger was also returning, and it was good to let it feed on the particular hate I had for this one man.

That removal of the blindfold had come as a surprise, because I had been sure that this man never wanted me to see his face. It very rapidly occurred to me that it was a signal of impending doom: that it mattered not, now, if I were even able to count the hairs on his head - the dead impart little direct knowledge.

He was of similar height to most Andean men, though his skin was lighter than the physiognomy would have suggested. I thought he was probably townbred, with some Spanish blood perhaps close to the surface. His hair was straight and black, what I could see of it under a felt hat. He wore wool trousers and a thick wool jersey, but his feet were not in the all-common sandals. He had black boots, as any ex-army officer might wear. A rifle was slung over his shoulder; spare magazines evident in the bulges of his trousers. A knife sat on his belt. But only in his eyes could I see anything that matched the voice, and which gave me something to describe to Tarrasco: they looked dead. Somewhere, this man had been defeated.

`Still serving?' I wanted to needle him, somehow not caring now that my own road was becoming critically short.

`Serving?'

In my tiredness I'd chosen a poorly translated term, and he'd not understood.

`You're still in uniform.'

`You're insane.'

`Fancy boots.'

`Deje de hablar porquerias.' Stop talking shit.

`You're still in the army.'

In that starlight I could see the sneer that crossed his face. `Like hell I am.'

`Have knife, will travel.'

It came out of its sheath with barely a whisper, the starlight kissing it with white beyond black. `Then let it touch your throat - you'll feel only its absence once it's gone.'

But I was coming to know my man, and the knife stayed sufficiently far from my throat to confirm his subservience to another. `How many, Capitán?'

'How many *what*?'

'Throats.'

'*Por Dios*! How should I know?'

'So many?'

'*You think I want to count?!*' And for the first time in hours his voice raised above a whisper, breaking the night with its desperation.

Shortly after he shouted his last words at me, he turned, and we continued our march across the *puna*. The path remained as difficult as before, though now he left me to his men whenever I fell, who just picked me up and pushed me forward. He seemed sunk in his own thoughts, paying less attention to the night around him, walking forward with less caution than before.

Perhaps two hours later I saw the shapes of some huts take form over the lip of a valley, and we stopped at the top of the slope while he took in the view ahead. Some sense of danger must have come back, for he took his time looking at each feature, paying attention to areas of greater shadow, depressions big enough for their closer slope to be invisible. After a while, clearly uneasy, he just grunted. '*Vamonos*.' One of his men prodded me.

It took a moment to put one foot in front of the other. Those huts had clearly framed themselves in my mind as our destination, and our pause on top of the hill seemed to me to be the last moment of rest and peace that I might ever know. To go down that slope was to walk right onto the knife he had, finally, after that shout, laid against my throat, before turning away.

There were no lights visible, and as we approached the dwellings he stopped us all before waving to one of his men on towards a hut that lay to one side of the community. I felt a hand on my shoulder, and though it applied very little pressure, there seemed to be little resistance in my knees. I folded slowly, falling forward on my elbows. A cloth came back, wrapped tight against my mouth, then forced between my teeth. The message was very clear.

The small figure slipped ahead, circling the hut from the side, then edging carefully towards the door. From where I lay I could see his head and shoulders above the coarse grass. He stayed unmoving for a moment, back against the wall, then pushed at the door with his gunbarrel. It opened without a sound, and after apparently listening to the darkness within the man dropped from sight. He reappeared about half a minute later, framed by the doorway itself, walking towards us. My guide nodded and I was pulled to my feet again.

The hut was empty of life, though it was so dark inside that I could not make out whether it was normally inhabited. A shove sent me falling against one wall.

` Stay there. And don't think about another shit. You don't have the time.'

The message was irrelevant, my state of dehydration severe enough that the body was no longer pulling fluids from the tissues to flush out whatever bacteria were still fermenting in my gut. I was shaking like a leaf, and even the last statement did little to add to the tremors. I lay, feeling a lead-like exhaustion throughout, and, without any evidence of its coming, slipped into sleep.

'Despiertese, señor, despiertese!,' Wake up, wake up! A hand was shaking my shoulder. It appeared to be one of the capitán's men, though it was still too dark to be able to see clearly.

I was still groggy with sleep, so full consciousness was still some way off. 'Let me rest.'

'You must get up now,' he insisted, 'otherwise we'll be too late.' His Spanish was the Spanish of a campesino but I understood him well enough.

'Where are we going?' I could read the urgency in his voice.

'I have to get you out of here before el capitán comes back.'

I wondered where *'el capitán'* had gone, but didn't realize that I had done so out loud until the man answered me.

'Ábajo, below,said the campesino.

' Abajo donde,' below where, I asked.

'Hasta la selva', as far as the jungle, said my companion.

'Cual hay en la selva?' What is there in the jungle, I asked.

'El General,' he said.

'El General?' I asked, fully awake now.

'Una patrulla,' a patrol, he said.

'Como sabes,' How do you know, I asked.

'Se lo dijeron,' He was told.

'Y tu?' And you?

'Me pagaron,' I was paid, he said.

Which set me back, as I was convinced that no-one cared. But either Carlos or Tarrasco had got to him with some money, enough to make a difference.

At that moment two things happened. The first was not good, because the familiar face of the capitán entered the hut. He took everything in with a glance, and began to draw something from his jacket pocket. His knife, I thought. Nor was the second, because directly over his shoulder I saw the Generalísimo. His face was as bloated and crimson as I recalled but lacked the sweat of his lackey, so I assumed he'd arrived by vehicle.

' Ah, the journalist', he said. And in a rapid aside he said something to his man that, as his voice was low, I didn't catch. Something to do with disposal, I presumed. He said 'So, did you find your story?'

I knew it was too late, then, because any smart answer of mine required Tarrasco coming through the door right now, and there was no sign of him.

Neil Thomas

Ghosts

The orange and yellow fingers of the fire wave in the slow air currents of the hearth, reaching as far as they can into the night of the chimney above. The baulks of wood hiss and steam, releasing occasional jets of flame quite different from the lazy display lapping above. A slight warmth reaches across the room, but is not sufficient to penetrate the chill that seems lodged in my very bones. It is a chill that has been upon me as and since I returned, a ghostly wrap that refuses to release me even into the frigid winter air outside the house. I recognize it as a burden to be borne for some time yet.

The house is as I left it, as if it were only yesterday that I switched off the light behind Grandfather's chair before moving to the hotel. But in those seven weeks a world has come and gone, and it has put Grandmother's passing plainly behind me. Now, I do not miss her I did before, that keening sense of loss which made itself felt so strongly that I thought it could never depart. No; now, she is a memory, someone who made my life something to be lived, someone who, even if belatedly and indirectly, knew how to show me the difference between right and wrong, and left me better than before. I accepted and learnt the lesson. I sit in Grandfather's chair and let those thoughts flow through me. And recognize that in the life that is still mine I have a whole world before me to look at and think about.

I came back here because I felt that it was a homecoming. I had survived it all; I had a right to come home. Now, perhaps, there is a need for some reflection. But that chill makes it quite clear that I should not exult in my survival. Others did not survive. So I carry their ghosts with me.

I carry many ghosts. The last memory I have of my parents is lit by that Mediterranean light which washes walls already white and makes them seem translucent. The room is large and the three of us are sitting, looking for words. Perhaps that is not strictly accurate - I am waiting for some, believing that I have a right to be spoken to. But the conversation avoids me, flows around and over me like some drumlin under the weight of a glacial anger that is the root of all they seem to say. They look for ways to avoid dealing with my presence.

As a thousand times before, I tire of waiting. My interjections, wedges designed to open hairline cracks (the ice is too hard for a major fissure), are dealt with more by grunts or laughs, both sounds which probably occurred at least once at great depth in some previous ice age. Eyes look elsewhere, and cut-glass tumblers touch lips more interested in transporting the rest of the body to a higher, ethereal, alcoholic plain. They don't even look at each other.

But perhaps that is all a dream, too. For I don't really remember the last time we were together.

I pass two days, cleaning the house, looking at and touching what I have been left. Each room, some of them not very familiar, empties its store of memories. The house is practical, even if it is old, and I wonder what I can do with it. It is too big to live in by myself.

I am still not ready for company, so I take myself for long walks, avoiding paths that I think acqaintances might tread. Sometimes this involves the train, a day trip to Montreal and an excursion through the old port, or a short ride to the west and hours of frozen rural roads past farms where only occasional gray-haired occupants speaks to the emptying of the land. Sometimes I find a library, because there are other thoughts developing, and I find myself ignorant of the facts that seem relevant. But in this period solitude is necessary, so human contact is nothing more than the occasional touch of a shop cashier's hand, the smile of a waitress, or the frown of a librarian wondering why I'm interested in something so odd.

A holiday Monday I happened on a pipeband. It would take a great stretch of imagination to describe a pipeband as polyphonic - if all the drones are perfectly tuned then it is just a single continuous chord that provides the counterpoint to the warbling chanters. Somehow, in the swaying kilts of the regimental band marching down Princess Street, I saw the tunics of equally cold, massed Roman legionnaires traversing Gallic mountain passes. Then I was cast right back into that herd of alpaca in another mountain setting. Could they, I wondered, or anyone else, have understood how close I heard them once come to humming the pibroch of Donald Dubh?

I found Glasgie by coming to it from Gouverneur. At first I'd thought I was on a road to nowhere, for it wound through a fractured landscape, potholed itself, passing small farmsteads that could never have been more than a subsistence from nature. The sun was setting, and it shone right into my eyes, coming and going as I wound up and down, in and out, crest and dale. Then, as I came to a village, and saw the bridge over the river ahead, the hill to the left was alive with evening warmth. I turned my head and saw the buildings.

At first I could not believe they were ruins - they were magical in the evening sun, three-storied fieldstone, alive with the land around. But they were roofless, window glass long gone, and in some places the walls were beginning to collapse. I stopped and stood for a while at the falls, watching the waters that had given the energy to keep men employed. The empty window bays filled for an instant with all the faces of those that had ever entered the ironworks, then they were as stark as they had been for a hundred years, drained of any humour or passion they had once contained.

The knowledge that the walls could never be brought back to life, as could not any of those who had striven to build them, closed the day as firmly as did the sun as it left the small valley. I turned, and the river was black and cold as I crossed it, the small church beyond firmly closed against a taunting, early mist.

The road out and on to Oxbow and Theresa was smooth and kempt, and I vowed that I would never return by it for it had no spirit. Different from Cameron's time, when the valley would have been alive.

Ashes

About a week later, and quite late in the evening, there was a knock at the door. It was a cold, still night, and earlier, through the livingroom window, I'd seen the previous night's layer of snow in the street hardening into that larger-grained crystalline texture that comes after a strongly sunlit day. Chimneys gave off vertical plumes of feathered smoke which disappeared quickly.

I opened the door to find Angela standing there, wrapped in a heavy coat, fur hat pulled well down over her ears, hands dug well into her pockets.

`Hullo.'

She nodded. `I thought it was about time someone looked in on you.'

I stood back to give her room to enter, but she didn't move. `You mean...........? No, come in, first. You'll freeze, out there.'

She made it look as though she was thinking about it, then slowly stepped in. I shut the door behind her. She looked around, at a house she hadn't been in before, taking it in as someone at an auction peruses what's on offer, slowly, considering. `So. You came home.' She gestured around her. `You must be comfortable here.'

I could see and feel that she was hurt. `I had to work *out* where I was before anything else. I've been trying to come to terms with things.'

She shrugged. `Well, let us know when you've done it.' She turned as if to leave.

`No, Angie. Please. This isn't anything about you. This is about everything else. All that stuff I was dealing with when I left. I had to sort through it.'

`Where have you slotted *us* - Dad, Penny, ... me?'

I shook my head. `I haven't slotted anybody anywhere.'

159

'Then it didn't work.' Not a question. 'How long is it now, about two months?'

'About that. How did you know?'

'You forget where I work. I just let it be known that I'd appreciate the occasional report on the house. No break-ins, that sort of thing.'

I shook my head at myself, trying to loosen the fog that seemed gathered around my mind. I hadn't thought that anybody would be looking out for me. 'Let me take your coat. Please come and sit down so that I can explain.'

Her shoulders stayed a little hunched as I took her coat, tucking her hat and gloves into a sleeve. After hanging it in the hall closet I pointed to the living-room. 'Let's go in there.'

Perhaps the warmth of the room, both in the fire and in its spirit, thawed her, for she let her shoulders slump a little. I let her choose which of the two chairs to take, wondering which it would be. 'I think you need a drink. Something warm? Or a drop of something?'

She looked up at me. 'Warm.'

I nodded. 'Just give me a minute, then.'

Her look said: *One more won't hurt, now.*

In fact, it was several before I went back to the living-room. 'Hot buttered rum.'

She smiled wryly. 'Thank you.' She was still sitting forward in the chair, knees together, peering into the fire.

'Do you see anything there?'

'In the fire, you mean? No, not really. The flames are soothing, that's all.' She took a sip of her drink.

I took a sip of my own, looking for words to heal what was evidently a serious breach, but nothing of significant import came immediately to mind. 'Angie, you may not understand me, or what I've done, but when I came back I felt that it would be wrong to walk up to your door and move back in. I was there initially because of David's hospitality. Also, if I am honest, because I didn't have the courage to stay here.'

She said nothing, but just clasped her mug with both hands.

`I came back from Peru with some difficult things still to resolve. I felt that I shouldn't burden you or David with those. I needed to feel.......*landed*, to have come down to earth in a way that said I'd put something behind me, which I wouldn't have to think about again. But I was thinking about myself. Very selfish, perhaps.'

Her eyes accused me. `You forgot that when you went away you were going into danger, that...... perhaps...... we would be worried about you. When I worked out that it was you in this house, I wondered what it was that we'd done to make you feel that you couldn't come back to us. Oh, I don't mean me personally - I mean *us*, as a family. As the days went by and we didn't hear from you I just assumed that we'd been written off. I came tonight just to settle the matter.' She went back to the fire, angry, but sad, too.

I think that if I'd tried to find more excuses, she'd have been gone within five minutes. It came through to me that she was completely right, that I'd been thoughtless beyond forgiveness. I think it was because I'd spent so many years by myself, generally moving from hotel to hotel, that I'd become divorced from the warmer elements of human nature. No doubt my parents hadn't helped, but I couldn't blame it all on them. So, as I'd said, I'd thought about myself, thinking it more important to right that particular tangle of confusion before I gave consideration to anyone else.

Perhaps the rum helped a little, easing some of the tension under my diaphragm. Or perhaps this was what I'd waited for, without knowing that I was waiting. Angela was. I had promised her this, my story, but I didn't know how to start. Whenever I thought about the Andes, I first thought about the women, but, I thought, this isn't about women, this is about me, and him. But then I saw how to do it. 'All the Andean women I met,' I said, 'seemed to be ....'

All the Andean women I met seemed to be permanently attached to the ground beneath them. Their movements were always measured, never hurried. It was as if their existence could be threaded on a string, that string being the preordained path through a swamp of poverty and exhausting labour from which there was no exit. Thus they knew perfectly where they were going, only needing to harbour the strength they could for those moments which God or gods decided should test them.

The men, by comparison, could open doors from that path. And even if the occasional vista offered were not one that I would have considered very different, they, at least, had the possibility of choice. Which door was it, I wondered, that my captor had opened and had decided to take?

For in a way he had the measured steps of the women. The door taken seemed far behind him, and it was he who was now wading through a swamp, perhaps partly of his own making, perhaps not. He never became animated, except from anger. He expressed no interest, except for caution. This moment seemed no different from that, though I should have expressed such disinterest as languor rather than boredom.

After that night-time walk I assumed that I had little time left before whatever final fate was to befall me. I was not confident of a positive outcome, and, in the ensuing few hours as I thought about it more, knowing that positive meant alive, I recognized that even were there to be something called positive, it could have many faces. I desperately wanted the one that reason suggested was the hardest of all - full health.

Reason was something in itself which I thought would be lacking in that final moment. I'd seen the result, in other places, of the complete loss of reason in a mob - at that moment, humankind could be the cruellest animal of all. It mattered not to a mob to what or how it brought death - death was itself the purpose. Would it be different to my captor, who was after all a singular killer?

'And then, when I lay in that hut, almost identical to the one where those people were murdered, I saw far beyond anything I'd ever seen before. Not any sort of religious awakening or spiritual revelation, more just a blinding flash of understanding. I think if I'd not met Cameron it wouldn't have happened - I'd have been some sort of statistic somewhere, and nothing else. But, you see, I was him and he was me, and I knew that I could go forward without any worry at all about how it would end.'

`You thought you were safe?'

`No, no. I didn't care if I were safe. No, I just knew that I could take anything they wanted to give me, and if it meant that I died, well, so it would have to be. It was something totally different from the guilt I carried before. That was a terrible burden, a weight - *this* made me weightless. It was like a catalyst - it made me *eager* to know.'

I slumped back in the chair, exhausted. Another catharsis borne by Angie, I thought, but far different from the previous one. It had taken me an hour to get this far, an hour of taking her through it all, even the *chakitaklia*, to the point where they'd put me into that hut. She'd only spoken that once, at the end, to clarify something that I'd not put clearly. As I'd talked, her eyes had come slowly up from the fire, and then she'd watched me continually, watching the feelings as much as listening to the words.

'But you got away somehow. You're here.'

'Tarrasco brought me back to Carlos.'

'But, I thought you said.......'

'I said that he didn't come through the door when I thought I needed him to.'

'But he was there?'

'Oh yes. I just hadn't heard him arrive. That was his man that had tried to get me out of there.'

'But what happened to the general and the capitán. Didn't they get you first?'

'I'd made a mistake. It turned out that while he was López' man, his wasn't a military rank. They often call a village leader 'el capitán'. That's why it had stuck. But Tarrasco really was a major under the previous incumbent, and he was untouchable. The previous incumbent, you see, still outranked López in an army that owed allegiance to the current government, so López was going to do nothing that would see him demoted or transferred to somewhere worse. And Tarrasco had more men outside who outnumbered the men that López had thought to bring. And the bullet Tarrasco put in the capitán's head saved me.'

'So you were lucky.'

'If being saved by Tarrasco were due to luck, yes. But he and his men had, in fact, been just behind us all the way across the puna. He'd already known about the patrol, as nothing goes un-noticed up in the Andes, and this one had been under preparation for some time. He'd been outside, but required López to show his hand before coming in. With his men.'

I'm sure there were other questions spinning around her head, but Angie held her peace for a moment. Slowly she unbent from Grandmother's chair, and released a cold mug from white fingers. Then she just seemed to blur into the flames, those fingers apparently reaching out in the direction of my forehead, but I was asleep before any touch became evident.

`*Are* you well, Alastair?' David's question, with that specific emphasis, put his concern in a different realm from Angie's.

`Thank you, yes.' I paused. ` I hope I've made some amends, but it became clear last night that I've been little more than an idiot.'

He gave his gentle smile. ` I can't say that she came home happy, but I think she was less tense.'

I must have slept in that chair for several hours, for even though Angie had obviously banked it before leaving, the fire was just hot coals by the time I came around. I'd sat there for a few minutes, remembering, and had then gone to bed, sleeping the rest of the night more soundly than I had for weeks. I'd called David after breakfast, evincing the hope that he'd meet me in our customary coffeeshop.

'Did Angie say anything of our conversation?'

'Not really. More that your grandmother seemed to have worked some magic.'

'Grandmother? I wonder why she thought that? I didn't even mention her.'

'No? Well, perhaps she was looking at the greater picture. She saw that you'd come to terms with the house.'

'Yes. True,........ I'm sorry if I gave the impression that I didn't want to come back to yours. It was just that I felt leaving Peru as the first step in some sort of homecoming. Before, I was trying to cope with guilt and grief. It seemed impossible to separate the two. But Peru separated them completely for me, and I found myself coming home content with memories. The grief had gone.'

David nodded but said nothing. I knew that grief, for him, still brought its daily measure.

We both sipped some coffee, then he asked: 'What have you been doing since you came back? Are you writing again for the paper?'

'Not yet. I've made my promises in that direction, but I have another couple of weeks to put it all into perspective.' I thanked him mentally for not asking about Peru - I still felt the exhaustion of the previous night and was not sure that I could have been coherent beyond the point I'd got with Angie. 'I've been doing some research.'

Again he said nothing, leaving me to define the ground that we would tread.

'I had quite a bit of time to think whilst I was away. I decided that I needed to understand better how people lived before and during the 1812 war. Above all, how money was made.'

'Trade?'

'Yes. Who, and with whom.'

He waited. 'I've made hardly any progress with the trees.'

He meant the family trees. Thinking that had always been likely, I said 'Cameron hinted vaguely that there was greed behind his downfall. I found that I couldn't begin to understand what he meant without some knowledge of how people made money in those days.'

'Very carefully, I think.'

I knew that he meant that every penny would have counted in any transaction, because it was in some ways a very poor society - there was very little money circulating, and goods in general were not easily obtained. I nodded. 'Barter was generally the rule.'

'Have you a picture of it now?' Again, he meant trade.

'I think so - an axis of imports and exports along the St Lawrence from and to Montreal, with lateral flows on both sides of the border to and from this axis.'

'Yes, I think that's right.' He was kind enough not to tell me that he could have saved me a lot of reading. 'Other flows were far less important. The interior of New York and Vermont was difficult ground for movement of anything in volume. Water was still the key to trade.'

'So I found that Kingston was the main trading centre for Upper Canadians *and* Americans. In fact, commerce made a mockery of the whole conflict.'

David nodded his acknowledgement. 'The northern States hadn't wanted it - knew that they didn't have the resources for it.'

'So, to survive, they traded. To trade they smuggled. And there was little their own revenue officers could do about it.'

'Interesting picture, wasn't it?'

'Fascinating.'

'Perhaps it's hard to understand that, first, you had to come into this land with an axe. There were no open spaces. The early settlers were able to clear land at about four acres per year. It took them five to six years to create a farm - two acres for a garden and some twenty acres for crops, mainly wheat. During that time, there would have been few products that earned them an income - just wheat, pork and ashes.'

Our coffee had extended into lunch and David had just worked his way through a sandwich. We'd passed some sort of point at which I seemed to have reversed any fall from grace, and he'd talked about Penny, that she was a bit moochy these days - but he didn't lay that blame at my door. The sandwich seemed to have renewed his own thinking, and he'd started to talk about Upper Canada as it would have been in those days.

`Those three products are key to whatever went on. There was lumber as well, of course, but there was so much of it that it was steady revenue - not much potential for windfall profits.'

`Necessary for greed.' I meant the windfall profits.

David understood. `I think so. Now, the end market for each of those three commodities was quite different. The rapidly growing population, combined with the military presence, ensured that the majority of wheat grown stayed within the province. If not ground for flour it went to the small distilleries.'

`Pork?'

`The army was a major buyer of pork, and the war ensured demand.'

`Ashes seem a very odd thing to have traded in.'

`Ashes were the essential ingredient to many early industrial processes. Soapmaking, mainly. But they were, and remained, an export product. Fertilizer.'

'Potash'

'Yes.'

'Heavy stuff.'

'Yes.'

'I wonder if that is it?'

'What do you mean?'

'What was being traded.'

'Potash?'

'Yes. The forests of North America.' David was silent a moment. Then, 'It's a big leap, you know.' Alastair saw images of many falling trees in his mind, and of people sitting around, burning what they had felled.

'The hardwood forests of Upper Canada were on the move,' said Alastair.

'They were a settler commodity,' said David. 'Ashes paid for the clearance.'

'Only if there was trade,' said Alastair, 'and an inexhaustable European market.'

'The Canadian portion would have gone through Monteal.'

'All of Upper Canada in a barrel,' said Alastair.

'And that's what he was hanged for,' responded David.

'Cameron? Saw too much of a King's ship. What if...,' said Alastair.

'What if, what,' asked David.

'No. Just a thought. Genealogy again,' said Alastair.

'Genealogy?'

'Yes. What if there was an indirect betrayal by one of those named, oh, I don't know, some loose talk at a dinner given for visitors.'

'Yes, and.....?' David was still lost.

'Someone got to know what somebody else was up to.'

'We'll never prove it,' said David.

'No. We never will.' said Alastair.

Neil Thomas

Loose Ends

I thought in the end it didn't matter. There were only so many records, and it was a war that was receding rapidly into the past. Fewer records every day, and fewer souls to interpret them. It didn't matter who was whom, and who had done what. I knew that there was no way of uncovering what Cameron had got himself into, beyond the official story, and that there were as many interesting stories buried at Sandy Creek as there were men. These also disappeared into the past.

I had apologized to whom it mattered most, Carlos, Tarrasco, some Andean peasants, and still had some apologies to make to others, Grandfather, Grandmother, Angie, but I thought I owed Cameron one as well, as it was now too long ago to uncover the truth. And what did I think of Yeo and Chauncey? Not much, if the truth were known, but they were men of their time, who thought that victory depended on size.

I saw Fred Webster shortly afterwards.

'Hullo, Alastair.'

'Fred'

'I'm afraid it's probably not news you want to hear,' he said.

'Try me,' I said.

'Well, your Grandfather had done some genealogical research which went nowhere.'

'How do you know?'

'I was right about the coding, and all I found was family trees,' he said.

'Why had he coded them?'

169

'To stop them falling into the wrong hands, I suppose.'

I could only imagine that he was thinking about Grandmothers' but said nothing. There must have been some disagreement there.

'Never mind, Fred.

'Sorry, Alastair.'

I had been fooled by the diagrams. I saw that Fred had mounted his transliterations on cards, which looked very much like David's early genealogical work. So Grandfather had hit the same roadblocks as David. And it made no difference whether a family line made it to the present day or not. I had to deal with two-hundred-year-old actions.

I needed to find Macdonell's papers and thought that the library at the Royal Military College was the place to start. It took an hour to be processed at the library, but I had the run of the place after that. It took me two further hours to run down a card, which told me to see the Cartwright collection at Queen's if I wanted anything more, and as it seemed that I had exhausted RMC's store of two-hundred-year-old artefacts, I headed back to Kingston for lunch. I spent the whole afternoon with Cartwright, and learnt a lot about his business. At one point I even had him down for Cameron's betrayal, for I suddenly came on mention of potash, but the date was wrong. Nothing on Macdonnell. Anywhere. He must have gone back to New Brunswick, where he came from.

I returned to that chair opposite Grandmother's and, for the first time in months, poured myself some *fino*. I needed to think about what I was doing and what I wanted from it. I thought the *fino* might help me get there. Firstly, I had to decide whether there had been disagreement between Grandmother and Grandfather over the family trees. If there had been, I could only think that was because Grandmother thought it an unnecessary diversion. The binary code I put down to Grandfathers' idiosyncrasies. But if Grandmother thought it an unnecessary diversion, that meant she had worked through what had really happened. So I left Grandfather there, between the old ashes of the fireplace and the dregs of the fino.

Then I had to come to terms with what I thought Grandmother really knew, and that was a far harder puzzle. There was nothing I had found that she had written. It was all gone now, anyway, consumed in that fire that took everything but the diaries and one or two things of Grandfather's that I had been working on at the time. Then I decided that

Grandmother knew Cameron had been unjustly hanged, and that her purpose in all this was for me to work out why. That, after all, was why she had left me the papers. Therefore the question was, did she know as little as I did, or was I expected to find out a little more? In reality, we were both stuck. I had only advanced the story a little on the American side of the border. But perhaps that was all she expected, anyway, because as soon as you saw that there was an American dimension to this, the whole matter changed. I understood that Cameron had seen something he was probably not supposed to see, but I had only flimsy evidence as to what it was. I thought it unlikely that it was just about trading on a King's ship. But, if you added windfall profits from trading something like potash, perhaps it was a different story.

I went back to Cartwright's records and found that there was a period when his potash exports were lower than normal. As this coincided with the dates of the war, I'd put it down to the general havoc of the time, but his other business had grown, so it was unlikely that this was the reason. But if someone had come in and just wrested this business away, then that was a whole different kettle of fish. It seemed that he'd been excluded from cross-border purchases just when the war-driven supply was increasing. Yet the down-river supply kept growing, so there must have been another up-river source. This threw a whole new light on the intelligence needed to run a business, and the sacrifices that would need to be made to ensure that it kept flowing. It meant that knowledge was two-edged when it came to making money. I saw the reason for cross-river dinners.

Angie was at home giving Penny a bath when I called. 'We'll expect you for dinner, then,' she said.

David was there when I arrived, just home from a walk from Queen's along the river. He looked at me surreptitiously. 'You look as though you've come to a decision,' he said.

'Several,' I said.

'Tell us over dinner,' said Angie, still a bit distant.

Dinner smelt not far away, but David still offered some wine to bridge the gap.

'Red, please,' I said.

He poured the same for all three, passed Angie's and mine, and then toasted, 'To decisions made,' he said.

I felt awkward, because I thought the decision(s) was mine alone, but then saw that I was wrong. 'To decisions,' I said. Angie was quiet. David saw this, but said nothing. He led us to the chairs, and sat in one. 'You might as well begin,' he said.

I thought a moment. Then 'Grandmother set me a task. I saw this as a challenge, rather than as a collaborative venture, which might have been better. I also assumed that I was adding knowledge rather than just adding slightly to a dimension. It's quite possible that she knew what had happened. I'm not sure I know much more, if even that. And it doesn't matter anymore.'

David made as if to speak, then decided not to.

'Oh, I used her initiative to help me out of the Peruvian mess, but the more closely I look now, the better I understand her motives. She was not setting me a challenge. She was introducing me to a forbear. One who had a grizzly end, I admit, but one whose history is inextricably linked to this place. As is this place to the border.'

'The border, now, or the border, then?' asked David.

'More then than now,' I said. 'But it should still be seen as relevant. It was to the 1812 population because it was the axis on which everything moved. It still does, though that is an outcome of the war, rather than a reason for it.

'So you have come down on the side of trade,' said David.

'Trade in something that could make someone a lot of money,' I answered.

'And those five names?

'As I suggested, I think one gave too much away while dining with Macdonnell and Foster's nephew was there. Cameron couldn't find out.'

'I'll just check the lasagna,' said David, and got up to go to the kitchen. They heard him getting plates ready.

'I think I'll keep the house,' I said to no-one in particular.

'Who is going to live in it?' asked Angie.

'Me,' I said.

And finally got a reaction.

'And the Toronto writing?'

'Can as easily be done from here.'

'But.....why.....?'

'I have a small girl I wish to see.'

Epilogue

The letters have only once seen light of day since they were put in the box. A sociologist skimmed them, looking for anything that might have elucidated his arcane thesis on incestual relationships within the [coal-mining] families of small rural communities in central Virginia. But the letter-writer was not even born and bred in the subject region, nor was he of [coal-mining] stock so could not have contributed to the research findings, no matter what he did. Typical of many academics, the sociologist wished to worry only a single bone, and so missed a different message. A hundred years already in those quiet archives (somewhere else the previous hundred), the odds that this message will ever surface again are slim.

Philadelphia,

My dear Sir,

I am in receipt of your favours of the 3rd and 27th ultimo, for which I must thank you. It cannot befall many young men to have the good fortune of such a benefactor as yourself, and were my mother alive today she would bless you, her brother, my dear uncle.

Since the General declared the vacancy of captain, and you secured of him my commission, my life has changed considerably. May I say I do not miss those days of idleness, even though the company of my peers was uncommonly good, and we passed hours in the pursuits expected of young gentlemen. But I know now that the tables always present risk and that there have to be moments of unluckiness. I must have been a burden to you, sir, given that my unluckiness seems, of late, to have been continuous. I thank you for having paid Mr Fullerton the £100 on sight of my note. I shall heed your latest advice to avoid further debt.

I hope it may please you that I was granted an audience with the General before my departure from Washington. During my presence he was in continuous conduct of the business of Secretary of War, but took moments to tell me of his fears for the northern frontier. I assured him I would do all in my power to harry the British where and when I could. I doubt that he remained uncertain as to my bravery and loyalty to the cause.

Here in Philadelphia all is haste. Even a nag commands a high price, and I must be able to horse well at least my junior officers. Could you find it in your benevolence, sir, to deposit a further £500 to my account? I must also find the wherewithal for uniforms, weaponry and even a signing bonus, for there is much recruitment in Philadelphia at present and if I am to raise a company in a short time I shall no doubt have to offer considerable inducement. The promise of British loot may not be enough.

Last night I had the pleasure of dining at Mr Hodge's table, and must thank you again, sir, for your note of introduction, for it showed me a gentleman of rare breeding and consideration. He was vastly interested in my mission, given as he has his own interests in that part of the north where I am eventually headed. He offered me an introduction to his own agent there, which I dare say I shall accept as I hear that it is a place still rather unsettled and backward. Even though I shall have my own troop behind me, I should not wish to lack refined company altogether.

I promise you, dear uncle, that you shall not find your nephew wanting. There are opportunities for glory in this war, and what better way for a young man to prove his worth than to win the battles put in front of him. Perhaps you will find mention of me in despatches, or on the front page of your newspaper as you peruse it over your breakfast table.

Please excuse this scrawl, but I am in haste to take my lunch.

Your Humble Servant, Sir,

Daniel Harris.

What can be said of this young man? Fond of expensive pleasures, perhaps, and looking for advancement according to the manner of most young gentlemen of his time. Perhaps he has not separated 'cause' and 'loot' very carefully, in terms of how honour might present them, but in this he appears little different from the warmongers themselves, to whom looting the northern frontier was itself the cause. Dishonest, also, because he had already been given a horse, but, no doubt, could find a good use for £500.

The next letter comes from South Carolina within the year, so the nephew must have resigned his commission fairly quickly. There is no word of the horse.

He died an unknown.

Made in the USA
Charleston, SC
30 June 2012